W9-BDA-183

election

election

a novel

TOM PERROTTA

g. p. putnam's sons
new york

G. P. PUTNAM'S SONS
Publishers Since 1838
a member of
Penguin Putnam Inc.
200 Madison Avenue
New York, NY 10016

Library of Congress Cataloging-in-Publication Data

Perrotta, Tom, date.
    Election: a novel / Tom Perrotta.
          p.   cm.
        ISBN 0-399-14366-1 (acid-free paper)
        I. Title.
    PS3566.E6948E43   1998   97-28785   CIP
    813'.54—dc21

Printed in the United States of America
10   9   8   7   6   5   4   3   2   1

This book is printed on acid-free paper. ∞

Book design by Junie Lee

I'd like to thank Janice Shapiro, Albert Berger, and Ron Yerxa for their enthusiasm and support. Thanks, too, to Maria Massie and Christine Pepe, and, as always, to Mary, Nina, and Luke.

"The teacher is engaged, not simply in the training of individuals, but in the formation of the proper social life. I believe that every teacher should recognize the dignity of his calling; that he is a social servant set apart for the maintenance of the proper social order and the securing of the right social growth."

—JOHN DEWEY

"The world is the School gone mad."

—WILLIAM TREVOR

for my brother and sister

MR. M.

ALL I EVER WANTED to do was teach. I never had to struggle like other people with the question of what to do with my life. My only dream was to sit on the edge of my desk in front of a room full of curious kids and talk about the world.

The election that turned me into a car salesman took place in the spring of 1992, when Clarence Thomas and Anita Hill were still fresh in everyone's mind, and Gennifer Flowers was the momentary star of tabloids and talk shows. All year long my junior Current Events class returned again and again to a single theme, what the media liked to call "the Character Issue": How are private virtue and public responsibility intertwined? Can you be an adulterer and a good President? A sexual pervert and an effective, impartial member of the judiciary?

It's fair to say that these questions interested me more than my students. Like most American adolescents, the kids at Winwood High didn't pay too much attention to the Supreme Court or the race for the White House. Their concerns were narrower — school, sports, sex, the unforgiving politics of the hallway and locker room.

But we also had the Glen Ridge rape case to discuss. My students were fascinated by this sad and sordid story, and it became the nexus where their concerns linked up with those of the larger democracy. The case had not yet gone to trial at that point, but the kids at Winwood knew the details inside and out. A group of high school athletes — the golden boys of Glen Ridge — had been charged with luring a retarded girl into a basement, forcing her to commit a variety of sexual acts, and then penetrating her vagina with a broomstick and a baseball bat. None of the defendants denied the event had occurred. Their defense was that the girl had consented.

We had developmentally disabled kids at Winwood, and we had football heroes, too; the gap between them was immense, almost medieval. It wasn't too hard to imagine how a lonely, mildly retarded girl might consider it a privilege of sorts to be molested and applauded by the jock royalty of her little world. They were the ones with the power of conferring recognition and acceptance. If they saw you, you existed.

Given the similarities between Winwood and Glen Ridge—we were only separated by a couple of exits on the Parkway—it didn't really surprise me that the overwhelming majority of my class, girls included, sided with the defendants and their right to a good time. If a girl, even a retarded girl, was dumb enough to join a troop of red-blooded boys in a basement, then who could blame the boys for taking advantage of this windfall?

I had my own opinion of the defendants—I wanted to see them convicted and sent to prison, where they could find out for themselves what it meant to be scared and weak and lonely—but I kept it to myself in the classroom, opting instead for the more neutral roles of moderator and devil's advocate.

"They were strong and she was weak," I pointed out. "So don't the strong have a responsibility not to hurt or humiliate the weak?"

Lisa Flanagan ventured the first response. She was exactly the kind of kid I was trying to reach, a smart, unhappy girl who wanted nothing more than to be accepted by the jock/cheerleader aristocracy at Winwood and had no idea—how could she?—of how relieved she was going to be to find a different world in college, more charitable standards of value.

"Mr. M.," she said helpfully, as if cluing me in to the true nature of the world, "that's not how it works. The strong take what they want."

I raised my eyebrows.

"Might makes right, Lisa? Is that what you're trying to tell me?" I pointed at Dino Mikulski, the steroid monster in our midst, a 285-pound brick of zits and muscle who already had major college football coaches drooling over their playbooks. "If you're correct in your analysis, then I move that Dino be declared President of the United States. I have no doubt that he could take George Bush in a fair fight and therefore deserves to be our leader."

Lisa got my point. Her face tightened with dismay as Dino and his lackeys exchanged high fives, celebrating his sudden ascension to the leadership of the Free World. I was pleased to see Paul Warren's hand shoot up.

"Those Glen Ridge guys are scum," he declared, silencing the room with the force of his judgment. "That girl didn't deserve what they did to her."

If I had to stick a pin in the map of the past and say, *There, that's where it all started,* I guess I'd choose that moment.

PAUL WARREN

IT WAS LIKE I'd just opened my eyes after a sixteen-year nap and was wide awake for the first time in my life, seeing things for what they were. I'd check out the news, and where it just used to be a blur of names and faces, now it was like, "Holy shit, people are *killing* each other. Little kids are starving to death."

Mr. M. was a big part of that. He wasn't your ordinary teacher, slouching in front of the blackboard, droning on about nothing for the whole period, the boredom thickening until it came to seem like a climate, the weather we lived in until the bell rang. He had a way of explaining complicated things so they made sense to you, connecting current events with familiar details from our own lives, asking questions that really made you think.

"*You've* all puked," I remember him saying one day. "I know I have. It's no big deal. People figure you're sick, or maybe you drank too much. But when George Bush loses his lunch in Japan, it's a national crisis. Now why do you think that is? What makes his vomit so different from yours or mine?"

Way more than Mr. M., though, it was the meltdown between my parents that snapped me out of my daze. There's nothing like your mom kicking your dad out of the house to make you play back the tape of your existence and see it all in a whole new light.

I'm like, *Okay, now I get it*. Dad wasn't working late. And Mom wasn't crying over those stupid TV movies. Our life was a soap opera, not a sitcom. And that whole time, with the clock ticking and our house waiting to explode, I was living in a dream world, grunting in the basement with Van Halen blasting, trying to bench two-fifteen, or hiding in my room with the Victoria's Secret catalogue, studying those pictures the way I should have been studying math. (Can somebody tell me why those women don't have nipples? It kind of drives me crazy.) My sister thinks I'm a moron for not catching on sooner. She and Mom are pretty tight; they knew about Dad and Sarah Stiller months before the news trickled down to me.

In my defense, I was preoccupied by major life questions. After football season, I took the PSATs along with everybody else in my class who wanted to go to college, and thought I did okay. But then the envelope arrives and it turns out that I got the third-highest score in all of Winwood High. At first I thought it must be some kind of computer error. I was just a B student, coasting through school with a minimum of pain and effort. For as long as I could remember, people had been saying that Tammy was the smart one in the family.

Those scores aren't supposed to mean that much, but they changed everything for me. I started thinking that maybe I could get into a decent college; maybe I could even make it through law school. Maybe I don't have to be a card-carrying corporate drone like Dad after all, another ant in the ant farm.

I'm sorry for Mr. M. I wish he hadn't done what he

did, especially not on my behalf. But I'm also eternally grateful to him for recognizing the change in me and encouraging me to act on it. The day he asked me to run for President was one of the proudest in my life.

MR. M.

PAUL WAS THE perfect candidate—varsity fullback, National Merit semifinalist, a good-looking, genuinely nice kid without an ounce of arrogance or calculation. He was smart, but unlike his sister Tammy, he didn't wear his IQ on his sleeve. In fact, if you didn't know him well, you could have easily drawn the conclusion that he wasn't the swiftest guy in the world, with that pumped-up body of his and those utterly vacant blue eyes.

I didn't bullshit him about service to school or any of that. As faculty advisor to the Student Government Association, no one knew better than me that the post of President was entirely ceremonial. All you presided over were a handful of meetings and a couple of bake sales.

"You're a smart guy," I told him. "But the admissions people at the selective schools are going to notice the gap between your grades and your board scores. The only thing that's going to convince them to take a chance on you is the right mix of extracurriculars.

Varsity sports look great on your application, but nothing beats President of your school. They really eat that up."

Paul blushed—he did that whenever anyone praised him—and lapsed into his mild stammer.

"Y-you think I can really win?"

"I don't see why not."

"But what about Tracy?"

"I wouldn't worry about Tracy. You're a lot more popular than she is."

TRACY FLICK

ALL RIGHT, SO I slept with my English teacher and ruined his marriage. Crucify me. Send me to bad girl prison with Amy Fisher and make TV movies about my pathetic life.

(If I'd been on better terms with Mr. M., I could have explained to him that my punishment for sleeping with Jack was having to sleep with Jack. It pretty much cured me of the older-man fantasy, let me tell you that.)

Until Paul entered the race, I was running unopposed. People understood that I deserved to win. They didn't necessarily like me, but they respected my qualifications: President of the Junior Class, Treasurer of the SGA, Assistant Editor of *The Watchdog,* statistician for the basketball team, and star of last year's musical (*Oklahoma!,* in case you're wondering). And I did all of it while conducting a fairly torrid affair with a married man, even if he did turn out to be as big a baby as any sixteen-year-old.

One of these days before I graduate and begin what I hope will be a brilliant career at Georgetown University, I'm going to get dressed up in high heels and a short skirt and head down to that Chevy dealership on the Boulevard. I'm going to ask for Mr. M. by name and make him show me all the shiny cars, the Camaros, Berettas, and Corvettes.

"What about gas mileage?" I'll ask him. "Tell me again about the antilock brakes."

I swear to God, I'll make him suffer.

PAUL WARREN

YOU ONLY NEED a hundred signatures to put yourself on the ballot. I'd accumulated eighty-something my first half hour in the cafeteria when Tracy came charging up to my table in those amazing black jeans.

"Who put you up to this?" she demanded.

Tracy's kind of short and moon-faced, but something about her gets me all flustered. It's pretty simple, really: she's got this ass. Just ask any guy at Winwood.

Conversations stop every time she walks down the hall. She wore these cut-offs last spring that people still talk about.

"What?"

"I asked you a simple question, Paul. Or do you expect me to believe that you just woke up this morning and decided to run for President?"

"I've been thinking about it for a long time."

She shook her head and smiled with pure contempt. I felt like I'd turned into a pane of glass.

"You're not a good liar, Paul."

She surprised me then by plucking the pen out of my hand and signing the petition.

"I've been working toward this for three years," she said, dotting the *i* in her last name with her trademark star, "and if you think you can just jump in at the last minute and take it away from me, you're sorely mistaken."

It's funny. She was trying to show me she wasn't scared, but the message I got was exactly the opposite. For the first time, I actually believed I might be able to win.

"Well," I said, reclaiming my pen from her sweaty fingers, "I guess we'll just have to let the voters decide."

MR. M.

THE ELECTION FOLLOWS an orderly, three-phase schedule. March is petition month. Any student can become a candidate simply by submitting a petition with the required number of signatures. The Candidate Assembly on the first Tuesday in April marks the official beginning of the race. The next two weeks are devoted to the campaign. The hallways and bulletin boards are plastered with signs and posters. Candidates greet their fellow students at the main door, passing out leaflets, shaking hands. *The Watchdog* publishes a special election issue. It's democracy in miniature, a great educational tool.

It's clear to me now that I was wrong to get so involved in Paul's candidacy. I don't think I admitted to myself how badly I wanted to see Tracy lose.

That girl was bad news, 110 pounds of the rawest, nakedest ambition I'd ever come in contact with. She smoldered with it, and I'd be a liar if I said I didn't find her fascinating and a little bit dangerous, especially after what I'd heard about her from Jack Dexter. She was a steamroller, and I guess I wanted to slow her down before she flattened the whole school.

My saving grace, or so I thought at the time, was simple: Paul Warren would make a terrific President. The office would be good for him, and he would be good for the school. And besides, he had as much right to run as Tracy did. Winwood High School was a democracy. The winner would be determined by popular vote, not my personal preference.

All the way through the last week of March, it looked like we would have a clear-cut, two-way race between Paul and Tracy, a race I had no doubt my candidate could win. So you can imagine my annoyance on March 29th when I walked into the cafeteria and saw Paul's little sister, a scrawny, morose-looking girl, standing behind a petition table, holding up a homemade sign.

"TAMMY WARREN," it said. "THE PEOPLE'S CHOICE."

2

PAUL WARREN

I'M NOT SURE what happened between Tammy and Lisa. They'd been best friends for a couple of years, but then they had a falling-out. When I asked Tammy about it, she screamed. I mean it. She threw back her head, opened her mouth, and shrieked. She couldn't have wailed any louder or more convincingly if a man in a hockey mask had attacked her with a meat cleaver. Mom came rushing downstairs like a maniac, holding the toilet bowl scrubber out in front of her like the Olympic torch, her right arm sheathed in an elbow-length orange rubber glove.

"Jesus," she told me. "I thought you were killing her."

Tammy likes nothing better than to persecute me and manipulate Mom. Now that she'd accomplished both goals in one fell swoop, a smile of angelic satisfaction spread across her face.

"Mom," she said, "would you kindly tell this *asshole* to get out of my face?"

Mom sighed, and I felt sorry for her, a tired-looking woman with a dead marriage who couldn't even clean the bathroom in peace.

"Tammy, do you have to use that word?"

"For him it's a compliment."

"Hey," I said. "Excuse me for living."

"Gladly," she said. "Just let me know when you get a life."

LISA FLANAGAN

I HONESTLY DON'T KNOW how I let it happen. It was like this huge mistake I couldn't stop making. I used to walk home thinking, *That's not me. That's not who I am.*

We were watching *Oprah* the day it started, this thing about women with implants. Mr. and Mrs. Warren were at work, and I guess Paul was at football practice. I remember gazing down the front of my shirt, shaking my head.

"I wish mine were bigger."

"Let me see."

"What?"

"Let me see. I'll give you an honest opinion."

Tammy and I had spent a lot of time together, slept over each other's houses, sometimes in the same bed. We'd seen each other with our tops off. It didn't make sense for me to be so nervous. I pulled the front of my shirt up over my face so she could look. She was smiling when I let it back down.

"You're okay."

"You think?"

She shrugged. "That bra doesn't do a lot for you."

"It's my mom's idea. She thinks it'll give me some shape. A little support. I keep telling her there's nothing *to* support."

"I don't mean that. It's just so plain."

"Who cares? Nobody sees it."

She peered at me through her glasses, her mouth puckering into this flirty little pout.

"*Somebody* might."

"Tammy," I said, my voice trailing off in a weird giggle.

"Wait here," she said. "I want to show you something."

She was gone for a couple of minutes. I tried to watch the show but I was too distracted.

"Close your eyes," she called from the bedroom.

"Come on, Tammy. Don't play games."

"I mean it. No cheating. Close your eyes."

I did what I was told. Tammy was younger, but she was always the one in charge.

"Okay," she said. "You can open them."

You have to understand that she isn't really that pretty. She's kind of mousy, and her body gets lost inside those huge sweatshirts she wears (they used to be Paul's, and some of them hang past her knees). Her hair is nice, brown with red-gold highlights, but she does it all wrong, this misplaced ponytail rising like a fountain from the top of her head.

"What do you think?"

Her hair was down and the glasses were gone. I knew from swimming that she had a cute figure, but the red silk heightened everything. Her skin seemed to glow.

"Wow," I said.

"I know." She bit her lip and looked bashful. "I stole it."

She turned around. The slip was so short it didn't really cover her butt. I couldn't believe I was looking at Tammy.

"Go in my room," she told me. "There's something for you on the bed."

The thing I found there looked like a transparent bathing suit, filmy black and weightless. Slipping into it was like climbing into someone else's skin.

"Turn around," she said from the doorway.

No one had ever looked at me like that.

"You're so pretty," she said.

My body felt hot, like there was this tiny sun burning in my chest, giving off light and energy.

PAUL WARREN

YOU WOULDN'T exactly call Lisa "cute." She's sarcastic-looking and her hair's too short. She's almost totally flat-chested and hardly ever wears makeup. Until she became my unofficial campaign manager, it never even occurred to me to think of her as a potential girlfriend. She was more the sisterly type, someone to tease and goof around with. But something changed between us that day in the cafeteria, when she glanced up at me while signing the petition.

"Paul," she said, "I think you'll make a *great* President."

It was kind of informal at first. We chatted in the hallway, ate lunch together, discussed various strategies for defeating Tracy. Then she asked me to come home with her one afternoon.

On her own initiative, she'd designed five sample campaign posters, each one featuring a pastel portrait of me, along with a slogan she wanted me to consider.

— A WINNER FOR WINWOOD
— A CHOICE, FOR A CHANGE
— THE RIGHT MAN FOR THE JOB
— TRUE LEADERSHIP
— PAUL POWER

The portraits were all slightly different. In one I wore a shirt and tie, in another my football jersey. "PAUL POWER," my personal favorite, was designed like a baseball card. Here I was grinning; there I seemed to be gazing into the distance. In every version, though, I had these deep violet eyes and a superhero jaw. Lisa saw me the way I saw myself in daydreams.

"Earth to Paul." She waved a sheet of paper in front of my face.

"What's this?"

"A draft of your speech. The Assembly's only two weeks away."

"Wow," I said. It was embarrassing to realize that she'd spent more time thinking about my campaign than I had. "I wish I knew how to thank you."

She touched two fingers to her mouth and gave it a moment's thought.

LISA FLANAGAN

TAMMY STARTED to scare me, or maybe I started to scare myself. It was like an undertow that kept dragging me farther and farther out to sea, away from normal life and other people.

We'd agree to stop, but then it would start right up again. It was hard to stay away from each other after school, when both our houses were empty and the only alternatives were TV or homework.

"When did you realize?" she asked me one day.

"Realize what?"

"You know. I've known for a long time."

I felt sick inside when she said that, like someone had accused me of a crime.

"I'm not like that," I snapped, my face heating with shame. "I don't even know what I'm doing here."

I moved away from her and began sifting through the tangled pile of clothes on the floor, trying to separate my stuff from hers. I spoke without looking at her. My voice shook.

"You think I don't want a boyfriend? Is that what you think?"

She didn't answer, but I heard her sobbing as I slammed the door. A week later I was back, modeling this pink camisole she'd stolen especially for me from Hit or Miss.

Once, at the movies, we sat far away from everyone and held hands. Sometimes she slipped little notes through the vents of my locker. She kept inviting me to sleep over in her bedroom, insisting that no one would ever suspect. I couldn't bear the thought, not with Paul and her parents in the house.

One day I noticed that a picture of me had appeared inside her locker, a snapshot from the previous Fourth of July. I was holding a hot dog in one hand and a burning sparkler in the other, looking happier than I actually remember being in my entire life. I ripped it off the door.

"You can't just keep that there," I hissed.

"Why not?"

"Someone might see it."

"So? It's just a picture."

"Tammy, please. Don't do this to me."

On Valentine's Day, when no one was looking, she gave me a red rose. She also placed an anonymous ad in *The Watchdog*.

"L.F.," it said. "Come watch *Oprah* with me anytime. Your totally secret admirer."

I have to admit, that made me happy. I must have read it a dozen times, thinking how nice it was to be remembered like that. All I gave her was a hard candy heart with a stupid message on it, "Sweet Stuff" or "Candy Girl," something like that.

Not long after that—I guess football practice got

canceled or something—Paul walked in on us in the living room. We weren't really doing anything, just watching TV with my head in her lap. She liked giving me scalp massages.

"Hey," he said. "Look at the lovebirds."

I sat up like a gun had gone off. I thought I was going to die, but Paul just went into the kitchen for a soda.

A couple of weeks later, somebody scratched the word "Dyke" into my locker. I remember staring at it for a couple of seconds, trying to catch my breath, feeling like someone had my head underwater and was holding it down. I knew we had to stop before something awful happened.

My solution was clean and dramatic. That spring, I joined the track team. Instead of spending my afternoons with Tammy, I occupied myself by running laps around the football field. I was cold to her at school and said I was busy when she called me at night. Eventually she got the message.

I liked running and turned out to be pretty good at it. The sunshine cheered me up and so did the fresh air and camaraderie of belonging to a team. Slowly, I started to feel like a normal person again, out of danger. Except sometimes, running in a meet, I had this creepy feeling she was chasing me, that I'd glance over my shoulder and see her bearing down, gaining with every stride.

TAMMY WARREN

I SAT in the bleachers and watched her run. She seemed so far away from that perspective, a total stranger, talking and laughing with her teammates, pretending not to notice me. They'd hug each other after crossing the finish line, three or four girls linked together in a private circle, sealed off from the world.

I felt so bad and weird that I actually made an appointment with the school psychologist. She's pretty, maybe thirty years old, with really great taste in clothes—silk scarves, Italian shoes, some kind of subtle perfume (most of the other women teachers smell like they're wearing Wizard room deodorizer). I remember walking into her office and wanting to *be* her, to skip ahead ten or twelve years to a time when I'd be poised and elegant and totally in control of my life.

"This is all strictly confidential," she told me. "Feel free to say whatever's on your mind."

"I'm in love."

Just blurting it out was such a relief, I immediately burst into tears. She pushed a box of Kleenex across the table and watched me with a sympathetic expression.

"Take your time," she said, pausing for a second to admire her enormous diamond engagement ring. "When you're ready, you can tell me all about him."

That's when I realized how impossible it was, my

whole life. Talking about it wasn't going to change anything. I thanked her for her time, and got a pass back to study hall.

PAUL WARREN

MY EX-GIRLFRIEND WAS a kisser. I went out with her a whole year and never even unhooked her bra. She was perfectly happy to make out for three hours at a stretch, but if I so much as tried to untuck her shirt, everything came crashing to a halt.

"*Paul,*" she'd say in this shocked voice, like I'd just whipped out a pair of handcuffs. "What are you *doing?*"

I guess that's why I was so amazed when Lisa started unbuttoning my shirt after just a few minutes of kissing. Her mother was at work, and I realized pretty quickly that she wasn't fooling around. Her face was hot and she was breathing in these hard little gulps. She took my hand and pulled me toward her bedroom.

"Are you sure?" I asked.

She said yes. She fumbled for something in her dresser drawer and told me she'd be right back.

Time seemed to expand while I waited for her, but I felt totally focused, totally connected to the moment, the way I did sometimes on the football field.

"Close your eyes," she said from the hallway.

TAMMY WARREN

I FOLLOWED THEM to her house. I sat on my bike by the mailbox and waited.

Now I knew how Mom felt the day she found out about Dad and Sarah Stiller. It was a complete coincidence. She'd taken off the afternoon to drive me to the eye doctor. On the way home, we happened to pass the Arrowhead Motel just as Dad walked out of the office.

Mom pulled into the parking lot of Giant Carpet, just in time for us to watch them slipping into room 16. Dad held his hand on her big butt and glanced furtively from side to side like a criminal. He looked so pathetic, a potbellied guy in a tweed rain hat, about to do the nasty.

Our original plan was to wait there until he came out, but Mom changed her mind after a few minutes, maybe because of me, I don't know. We drove home and she cooked dinner, just like any other night. Dad got home at six-fifteen, kissed her on the cheek, asked me about school. They stayed together three more miserable months.

I didn't chicken out like Mom. I forced myself to stay and watch. Two hours passed before Paul finally emerged from Lisa's house, blinking like the sun hurt his eyes, but by that time, I'd already decided to run for President.

3

MR. M.

THE CANDIDATE ASSEMBLY usually ranks as one of the duller rituals of the high school calendar, full of the windy rhetoric of commencement, but without the sense of festivity and true accomplishment that makes the excesses of graduation speakers so forgivable, and sometimes even touching.

I knew better than most people how little to expect because I had read and approved all the speeches in advance in my capacity as SGA advisor. I'm told that this custom of prior review dates back to the early seventies, when an honor student shocked the Administration by running on a pro-marijuana platform, and received a standing ovation.

"A joint in every locker!" he was supposed to have pledged. "Two buds in every bong!"

The speeches of 1992 looked to be nowhere near as interesting. Tracy Flick focused on herself, of course, her many talents and accomplishments, her proven ability to lead. Paul outlined a misty vision of a new kind of school, a cooperative, productive place without cliques or outcasts, an oasis of learning where students were equals in one another's eyes and teachers functioned as guides and helpers rather than narrow-minded disciplinarians. It was inspiring enough, but utterly beyond anything he had the power to achieve as SGA President.

Tammy was the wild card. On the morning of the Assembly, she submitted a woefully unfinished draft for my approval. It began with some interesting remarks about the school not meeting the needs of ordinary students, the ones who weren't academic or athletic superstars, but then it just fizzled out. The language was tentative and disconnected, and I remember thinking as I read it that she was in way over her head.

"Tammy?" I said. "Are you sure you want to do this? You can always try again next year."

She studied me through her glasses, and I thought for a second that she was ready to back out. But then she shook her head.

"No," she said. "I better go through with it. I think it'll be good for me."

Up to that moment, I'd been baffled by her candidacy, unable to see what an anonymous sophomore had to gain from competing head-to-head with an older brother who was a star athlete and one of the most popular kids in the school. But now I saw—or imagined—that she was doing it as a personal challenge, a way to move out of Paul's shadow and emerge as an individual in her own right. I knew the feeling, having spent my own adolescence locked in psychological combat with an older brother whose charmed existence always seemed to diminish my own.

"Can you finish this by seventh period?"

She nodded. "I'll work on it during lunch and study hall."

"Okay." I initialed the draft and slid it across the desk. "It's up to you."

TRACY FLICK

I THOUGHT TAMMY WAS a dweeby sophomore with some kind of weird death wish. From my perspective, she didn't alter the dynamic of the election at all. It was still me against Paul. Competence vs. Popularity. Qualified vs. Unqualified. Tammy was just a distraction.

LISA FLANAGAN

I WAS SO NERVOUS the day of the Assembly. It was my speech, after all, that Paul was going to deliver to the whole school. I didn't mind not getting the credit. Paul knew whose words they were, and that was enough.

In recent weeks, I'd become totally engrossed in the real presidential campaign and was learning for the first time about primaries, consultants, pollsters, spin doctors, all the behind-the-scenes players. I saw myself as Paul's strategist and chief speechwriter, his girlfriend and secret weapon, a cross between Hillary and Peggy Noonan.

We'd arranged to meet outside the auditorium before seventh period so I could give him my good luck charm. As soon as I saw him, I knew we were in trouble. He was pale with dread, and his lips had turned an alarming shade of blue, as though he'd been swimming for hours in icy water.

Two years earlier, right after my parents' divorce, my dad brought me on a trip to the Bahamas. The second or third day, we took a boat out to this coral reef where there was supposed to be fantastic snorkeling, big neon fish that swam right up and kissed you on the mask.

There were maybe twenty people on board, and when we got to the reef, everyone jumped in the water but me (I was mad at my dad and had decided to punish him by not having any fun). A couple of minutes later, this tall skinny man climbed back onto the boat and sat down across from me, still in his flippers and life jacket. He told me he was on his honeymoon and had had a panic attack the moment his face went underwater. His voice was normal, and I didn't realize how spooked he was until he tried to light a cigarette. His hands were shaking so hard he couldn't direct the match to where it was supposed to go. I had to do it for him.

Paul's hands were shaking just like that right before the Assembly. He reached up to fix his hair and almost missed his head.

MR. M.

HIGH SCHOOL STUDENTS are a notoriously tough crowd. They're suspicious of fancy rhetoric and sensitive to the slightest sign of self-importance. Raised on sitcoms, commercials, and MTV, their attention span for the spoken word is next to nonexistent. They arrange themselves in rowdy clusters and set their bullshit detectors on Red Alert.

Tracy understood this. Knowing she was a slightly ridiculous, slightly scandalous personage in the eyes of her peers, she decided to neutralize potential hecklers by emphasizing rather than soft-pedaling those aspects of her reputation. Sheathed in a startlingly short, body-hugging red dress and black tights, she delivered an unapologetic self-appraisal that was as accurate as it was provocative.

"I know you like Paul better than you like me," she said in summation, "and I don't really blame you. He's a nice, sweet guy and I'm a—well, I'm not nice and sweet, let's just leave it at that. But when it comes down to the wire, who do you want fighting for the students of Winwood High? Do you want Mr. Nice Guy?" She put her hands on her hips and smiled knowingly at the audience. "Or do you want me?"

TAMMY WARREN

I WATCHED PAUL and Lisa outside the auditorium. She was talking in a low voice; he was nodding. She smiled and touched him on the shoulder. He looked at his feet, shook his head. In two seconds, a total stranger would have known they were in love.

She held out her hand, a jewel-like crystal—her good luck charm—sparkling on her open palm. I ducked into the girls' room, found an empty stall, and stood inside it for five, maybe ten minutes, wondering

if I would always feel this bad, every day for the rest
of my life.

MR. M.

THE WHITE PAPER fluttered in Paul's trembling
hands. He stared down at the words with that troubled, mildly pained expression of his and spoke in a
barely audible monotone, forgetting to look at the audience.

"When you think about it," he whispered, "a school
is more than just a school it's our second home the place
where we spend most of our time and grow as individuals a community but is our school everything it could
be let me suggest to you that it is not . . ."

He stuttered, lost his place, omitted key words, went
back and read entire paragraphs over again. By the
time he reached the conclusion, even his most ardent
supporters were stupefied. Sound effect snores sawed
through the thick air, but Paul read on, undaunted.

"I want our school to reach its true potential a radiant city . . . uh, citadel of learning and serving I mean
service to humanity that is why I am running for President."

The applause that followed expressed relief rather
than approval, but I'm not sure Paul was up to making

that sort of distinction as he stood frozen at the podium in a post-oratorical daze, a grin of pure panic inching across his face as he tried to remember what to do next. The outgoing President, Larry DiBono, had to direct him back to his seat.

You had to feel for Tammy as she approached the microphone in a pretty flowered dress. The mob had grown surly after Paul's speech and was now eager for sport.

"Tammy! Tammy! Tammy!" they chanted, their wolf whistles and catcalls only serving to emphasize her plainness and obscurity. She had to climb onto a footstool just to see the audience.

LISA FLANAGAN

TAMMY DIDN'T SPEAK right away. She scanned the rows of seats spread out below her, as if trying to make eye contact with every single voter. I felt funny when she picked me out of the crowd and smiled. Suddenly there were only two of us present in that enormous room. I hated her for that, the way she still had of making everyone else disappear.

MR. M.

SHE MUST HAVE STOOD there for two solid minutes, letting the idiots have their fun. It was an extraordinary display of patience, something you might have expected from a veteran public speaker. When she finally opened her mouth, she had the undivided attention of everyone in the auditorium.

"Who cares about this stupid election?"

There was another eruption from the crowd, only this time it was spontaneous, cleansed of sarcasm. She had put her finger on the pulse of the event, uttered the unspoken truth that was hovering in a giant cartoon balloon over the entire gathering.

From his post by the emergency exit, the Vice-Principal, Walt Hendricks, shot me a startled glance. All I could do was shrug. She wasn't reading from the prepared text.

"You think it really matters who gets elected President of Winwood? You think it will change anything around here, make one single person happier or smarter or nicer? You think the food will taste any better in the cafeteria?"

The audience was quiet now, but it was a charged silence, the kind you'd get at a wedding if someone rose to tell the assembled guests exactly why this couple shouldn't be joined in holy matrimony. Walt flushed a bright dyspeptic pink and made frantic throat-slitting motions with his index finger, my signal to intervene. I rose from my aisle seat in the front row and began moving slowly toward the stage. I didn't want to pull the plug on the microphone, but didn't see much of an alternative.

"My opponents have a lot more experience than me," she continued. "But since it doesn't really matter, you might as well vote for me. Your lives won't be affected one way or the other."

I had my hand on the plug when she stepped down off her stool, crossed her ankles, and signed off, to a huge ovation, with a breathtakingly cynical little curtsy.

Walt's initial impulse was to banish her from the election, but I convinced him not to do it. I said it would turn her into a martyr for free speech and shake our students' faith in democracy. He was furious, though. Nothing bugs him more than insubordination from one of the "good" kids.

"The little bitch made a fool of us, Jim. We can't let her get away with it."

He suspended her for three days.

4

MR. M.

THAT SHOULD HAVE BEEN a happy time in my life. I had a good job, an apparently solid marriage, and an easy, unthinking faith in my own good judgment and moral integrity. Right now, that seems like more than enough to ask for.

I was restless, though. I thought about going back to school, earning a master's and maybe even a doctorate in Education, retooling myself for the administrative track. With all the ferment going on in the field, all the talk about the decline of America's schools and the need for a bold new generation of leadership, I sensed a golden opportunity for the transformation of my life.

After nearly a decade of classroom teaching, interacting with maybe a hundred kids a day, I was itching for a chance to apply my skills on a larger scale—

writing curriculum, formulating policy, developing innovative programs that would help reshape secondary education. I had visions of myself as a Principal, a respected authority on school reform, perhaps even a politician one day.

Measured against my dreams—which, admittedly, I'd done nothing to implement—my day-to-day life seemed a bit lacking. There were times when I nearly hypnotized myself with the drone of my own voice, the all-too-predictable trajectory of my classroom thoughts. I'd walk out at the end of the day feeling underutilized, like the best parts of me hadn't been engaged, and were turning rusty from disuse.

It's probably not surprising that this vague discontent spilled over into my marriage. There was nothing particularly wrong with it. For the most part, Diane and I got along well enough and enjoyed each other's company. We just felt stagnant, like a TV series that had run a couple of seasons too long. Part of it was that we were stuck in a holding pattern, trying to conceive our first child, but the problem ran deeper than that.

Diane has an enormous number of good qualities. She's attractive, well-read, politically aware, and good at her work (she does PR for St. Elizabeth's Hospital). People who know her consider her a loyal and caring friend, the kind of person you can count on in hard times and emergencies. After five years of marriage, her virtues were so familiar to me that I hardly even noticed them.

What I noticed more and more in the months leading up to the election were her shortcomings. There weren't many, but I guess I kept my eye out. Her underwear bored me. She ate an awful lot of ice cream that went straight to her thighs. She couldn't have told a joke if her life depended on it. She interrupted my reading. Sometimes I'd look at her and find myself thinking about Jack Dexter, wondering if I was finally beginning to understand.

TRACY FLICK

PEOPLE KEPT USING the term "sexual harassment" to describe what happened, but I don't think it applies. Jack never said anything disgusting and he never threatened me with bad grades. Most of our time together was really sweet and nice. I even cried a few times, it felt so good to have him hold me.

MR. M.

JACK WAS JUST like me. We started the same year at Winwood, and were friends within a matter of weeks.

We ushered at each other's weddings, played Friday night poker with a couple of his buddies, and made it a habit to get absolutely plastered once a year, on the last day of school. Both of us had electric guitars and vibrant fantasy lives, which we indulged every now and then in his basement, turning the amps up to ten and scratching out every three-chord anthem we could remember, plus a few that the world hadn't heard before.

The poker games ended in 1990, when Sherry Dexter got pregnant. I guess I wasn't too broken up about it. The games had gone from weekly to monthly by that point and had begun to emit the stale odor of rituals that have outlived their usefulness. But Jack acted as though something important and sustaining had been subtracted from his life. He started talking about poker all the time, wistfully, as if we'd been big-time professional gamblers instead of young married guys puffing on pretzel rods, biting our nails over a pile of nickels. If you asked about Sherry, he always said the same thing, with the same disheartened expression.

"She's enormous, Jim. Big as a frigging house."

Sherry was six months along when Jack started up with Tracy Flick. I know because he told me about it at lunch the next day, half bragging, half confessing his sins.

They were working late on the Valentine's Day edition of *The Watchdog,* just the two of them, when the conversation somehow turned to the subject of dating.

"The boys in this school are so immature," she complained. "They don't even know how to conduct a conversation."

"Oh?" said Jack. "So you'd prefer an older man?"

"As a matter of fact, I probably would."

"How old?" he asked, not quite teasing.

She pondered him and the question together.

"How old are you?"

"Me? Thirty-two."

"Thirty-two?" Her tongue made a thoughtful circuit of her chapped lips. "That sounds about right."

TRACY FLICK

IT SEEMED EXCITING to me, a new frontier. Jack had been flirting with me all year anyway, commenting on my clothes, telling me I reminded him of this girl he'd been in love with in college. He watched me all the time.

Yes, I knew his wife was pregnant. Everybody knew. Somehow that made it even more exciting.

It was the stupidest thing I ever did, but I wouldn't trade that first kiss for anything. And for all the trouble I caused him, I'd like to imagine Jack feels the same way, though I wouldn't blame him if he didn't.

MR. M.

I WAS APPALLED and jealous at the same time. I didn't want to lecture him, didn't want to offer even implicit approval, and couldn't quite conceal my curiosity.

I also had to accept a certain amount of responsibility. I'd been egging him on for years about the girls at Winwood, asking if he'd seen this one in her tight little skirt or that one in her black velvet top. Tracy had been a staple of our gossip for well over a year at that point. It was easier than you might imagine to forget she was fifteen. Spend enough time in a high school, and you forget what fifteen *means*.

TRACY FLICK

WE TOOK RISKS. Jack had lots of keys and more free time than I'd realized. He wrote me passes out of gym and study hall and we unbuttoned each other in musty storage rooms, surrounded by musical instruments, audiovisual equipment, shelves of mysterious chemicals. We did crazy things right in his classroom, in a corner you couldn't see from the door. I gave him a hickey one day under the stairwell, then painted it over with some cover stick. We fooled around in the darkroom, the handicapped elevator (this was after school, when the wheelchair kids had gone home), and backstage, behind the curtain. We kissed and licked and rubbed, driving each other crazy with our tongues and fingers. Twenty minutes of that and I'd walk around the rest of the day in a zombie daze, smiling at everyone I passed. It was the same for Jack. He forgot how to teach. He'd be standing there at the board and his face would just go blank. He'd tap the chalk against his forehead, leaving a cluster of faint white dots.

"I'm sorry," he'd say. "Where the heck was I?"

I was a sophomore. He was my first real boyfriend.

MR. M.

JACK WAS SIMPLY not functioning on a rational level. You saw him in the hallway with Tracy all the time, and he looked as love-drunk as any sixteen-year-old in the whole school. I expected to turn the corner one day and find them making out in front of her locker.

"Jack," I said. "This has got to stop. It's getting out of hand."

"I can't," he told me.

"You've got a wife," I reminded him. "A baby on the way."

"I know. But there's nothing I can do."

One Friday night in the middle of it all, Diane and

I had Jack and Sherry over for dinner. Sherry was big all right, but she seemed radiant and self-contained, stroking the hard dome of her belly as she spoke in a bright, authoritative tone about the pros and cons of midwives, birthing chairs, Pitocin, and epidurals. Jack sat beside her, jittery as a kid in church, his expression alternating between mild interest and profound boredom.

"Poor Jack." Sherry laughed and patted him on the knee. "He's heard all this a hundred times."

TRACY FLICK

IT HAD TO HAPPEN. The sex, I mean. It was our destination. We talked about it all the time as we touched each other under and through our clothes.

"I need to make love to you," he whispered. "I'll go crazy if we don't."

"Okay."

"Do you want it?"

"Uh-huh."

"Say it."

"Say what?"

"What you want."

"I want to make love."

"When?"

"Soon."

"Now?"

"Soon."

We came within an inch of it in the darkroom one Wednesday afternoon, but I made him stop. I didn't want it to happen like that, on a cold floor in a room that reeked of developer. We decided to play hooky the next day, to do what had to be done in a safe, private place.

MR. M.

SOMETHING HAPPENED, he never told me what. I guess Tracy came to her senses and decided to break it off.

Jack couldn't handle it. He put his hand through the windshield of his own car and ended up in the emergency room. He told Sherry he wanted a divorce. She was eight months pregnant at the time.

Despite Diane's vehement objections, he spent that night on our living room couch. I heard noises around three in the morning and went downstairs to check them out.

"Please," he said, in a voice not really his own. "I'm a friend of hers. I have an important message."

I turned on the light. He was sitting on the kitchen

floor in his underwear, a bottle of scotch cradled between his knees. His right arm was in a sling, the phone in his left hand.

"Jack," he said in that same harsh, desperate voice. "Just please tell her it's Jack."

TRACY FLICK

I HAD TO CROUCH on the floor of his Corolla until we pulled into the garage, a position that gave me ample opportunity to disapprove of his black sock / white sneaker combo. I'd never seen him out of school clothes before and had expected a sharper fashion sense than that.

It was interesting to wander through his house, to see how he lived when he wasn't at Winwood. A small, bright kitchen with a checkerboard floor and lots of new appliances. Pictures of three different babies stuck to the fridge by magnets in the shape of tropical fruit. I wanted to ask whose kids they were but he sort of steered me out of the kitchen, into a cozy den with Oriental rugs and a tiled fireplace. Magazines were scattered across a glass coffee table, just like in a doctor's office.

"This is where you spend most of your time, isn't it?"

"Huh?"

"You and your wife. You spend a lot of time in this room, don't you?"

He jammed his hands into his pockets and nodded. He looked tense and unhappy.

"Come on," he said. "Let's go upstairs."

At the foot of the staircase, I noticed this great little TV room with plush carpeting and a fat, comfortable-looking couch. I imagined us snuggling together in there, laughing at the nuts on Phil Donahue. There's something so luxurious about watching TV during school. You really feel like you're getting away with something. He reached around from behind and grabbed my breasts, squeezing so hard I winced.

"Come on," he said. "What are we waiting for?"

Two minutes later we're in the bedroom with our clothes off. The bed's unmade and the sheets smell like other people. There's a stack of baby books on the end table to my left—Dr. Spock, *What to Expect When You're Expecting*. This isn't what I had in mind, no more than the cold greasy floor of the darkroom. And suddenly I realize it: every time I've imagined sex for the first time, it's been in my own room, surrounded by familiar things—my stuffed animals, my Tom Cruise poster, the desk where I do my homework.

It's a bad dream: my English teacher is standing naked at the foot of this slightly lumpy bed, clutching a pair of not-quite-white underpants in his hand, studying me with this creepy look on his face, the one he gets when he's reading aloud in class and wants us to think he's moved by the passage.

"Tracy," he says. "Look at you."

How do I tell him I'd rather he didn't? That I've never been naked in front of a man and feel totally disgusted by my body? One breast is bigger than the other and there's a line of brown peach fuzz connecting my belly button to my pubic hair. It's kind of freakish.

To be honest, his body disappoints me, too. I know he's strong, but you can't really see the muscles. He's got love handles and no chest hair except these wispy little tufts growing straight out of his nipples. When he turns around to slip a cassette of middle-aged guy music into the boom box, there's a pretty big pimple on his butt.

He turns back to me and smiles. The clock behind him says 9:13. I belong in Psych, watching Mr. Farmer jam a knuckle up his nose while he drones on about laboratory rats. Next to the clock there's a wedding picture. Jack's wife looks pretty in her wedding gown, prettier than I'll ever be. Jack needs a haircut.

"Baby," he whispers, "I could die right now."

His penis grows before my eyes. I'm just lying there, wishing it was already over.

MR. M.

I ONLY SAW HIM once after he left in disgrace. He called out of the blue and asked if we could get together for a beer. I didn't have the heart to say no.

He stood by the coatrack at T.J. Peabody's, squinting in the direction of the bar. His face lit up when he spotted me, and I wished I'd never agreed to the meeting.

"Jimbo," he said, hoisting himself onto the stool beside me, greeting the bartender with a two-fingered salute.

"Jackie D.," I glumly replied.

The old nicknames were sorry reminders of better days: marathon jam sessions in the basement, end-of-the-year tequila blowouts, the night we forced a team of New York Jets into double overtime at a charity basketball game, amazing hundreds of Winwood students, as well as the Jets and ourselves.

He'd put on a lot of weight and looked pretty shell-shocked by his new life. He was back at his parents' house in Union Village, sleeping in his old bedroom, helping out at his father's hardware store, trapped inside routines he thought he'd escaped forever the day he graduated from high school.

"It's weird," he told me. "We eat the same food. The same shows are on TV. It's like science fiction or something."

I brought him up-to-date on recent events at school, the ordinary gossip that had once been the meat of our friendship but now only served to measure out the distance between us: Art Farmer had announced his retirement; Gene Sperigno and Adele Massing, two legendarily unattractive math teachers, had fallen in love in an after-school teachers-only bowling league and were planning to get married; Walt Hendricks had gotten arrested again for DWI, but somehow managed to get the charges dropped.

"Fuckin' Walt." Jack drained his beer, then held the mug upside down in front of his face to signal the bartender. "He knows how to cover his ass."

Thinking it might cheer him up, I told him about his replacement, a truculent ex-nun by the name of Marie Benson who had caused a mini-scandal by giving D's to half of her advanced sophomores.

"She has a bad stomach," I reported. "The kids call her 'Sister Mary Rolaids.' "

Jack didn't respond. He slurped the foam off his new beer and wiped his mouth with the back of his hand. His face grew somber in the mirror behind the bar.

TRACY FLICK

MY MOTHER'S ONE of those "involved" parents. She keeps pretty close track of my grades and stuff. One day she was going through my desk and came across my essay on *The Scarlet Letter*. Jack had given me an A-, corrected my spelling, and scribbled a note in red ink on the bottom of the last page: "Why won't you talk to me? Do you think love can be turned on and off like a faucet? Why don't you just get a gun and shoot me?"

That night, very calmly, she slid the paper across the kitchen table and asked me to please explain.

"Don't be scared," she told me. "I need to know the truth."

I broke down and told her everything. She hugged me and we both cried. The next morning we were in Mr. Hendricks's office. The day after that Jack was gone.

I feel bad for him, but I don't feel guilty. He was the adult. If he hadn't acted like such a baby, everything would have been okay.

MR. M.

"SO," HE SAID. "How's Sherry?"

"Okay. Things are still pretty tough for her."

"She won't talk to me, Jimbo."

"Can you blame her?"

He glanced up in surprise, stung by the sharpness of my tone. I wanted him to know that on this particular subject, I had no sympathy to offer.

"No," he conceded. "I can't blame her. But I would like to get to know my son."

I didn't know what to say to that. I'd held his infant son in my arms, changed his diaper, poked my finger into his plump little belly. I'd watched Sherry nod off while nursing and did my best to console her when she wept out of fear and frustration. Later on, I did even more than that.

"You made your choice," I told him.

"It's funny," he said, nodding in melancholy agreement. "I look at my life from this angle, and there's only one thing. All the college, all the teaching, all the years with Sherry, and all I was really doing was waiting for Tracy, so I could fuck it all up." He made a scribbling motion, as though signing an autograph. "*Slept with Tracy Flick.* That's my whole résumé."

I felt old when he said that. I looked at my tilted image in the mirror and had a strange premonition of my own doom.

"By the way," he said. "How's Tracy doing?"

5

PAUL WARREN

AT OUR STRATEGY SESSION that night, Lisa told me not to panic. Despite our setback at the Assembly, she thought the race had changed in ways that might ultimately work to our benefit.

"With three strong candidates," she said, "you don't need as many votes to win. We've got to shore up our base."

"Our base?"

"The voters we can count on no matter what."

"Who's that?"

"Jocks, cheerleaders, and wannabes."

"What's Tracy's base?"

"Not so broad. The AP crowd, maybe the band. But there are lots of people who think she'd make a good President."

"What about Tammy?"

She frowned. "I'm not really sure yet. But I think she'll get the burnouts and benchwarmers and the kids who feel left out."

Lisa was a natural at politics and the smartest person I knew (Tammy was a close second). I imagined her doing big things in the future, moving in important circles, worlds I would never know about. She'd be on a Sunday morning talk show, and I'd be sitting in my kitchen with a jelly donut, watching in amazement.

She said she loved me. We had sex every chance we got. But even so, there were times when I felt like her candidate first and her boyfriend second. She had this habit of floating away from me at crucial moments. A distant, distracted look would move across her face, and I could tell she'd forgotten me, and was thinking about the election.

TAMMY WARREN

PAUL LEFT for Lisa's right after supper, so it was just me and Mom again, as usual. Except it wasn't going to be a normal night. Mr. Hendricks had called her at work to explain about my suspension. He told me they'd had themselves "a nice little chat."

That was one of my ideas of hell, being discussed at

length by a leering, red-faced idiot like Mr. Hendricks. As far as I could tell, he earned his hundred thousand a year by wandering the hallway with a Styrofoam cup of coffee, smiling at the pretty girls and scowling at the boys who didn't play sports. Somebody should have stuck a broom in his hand and made him an honest man.

Mom turned off the TV in the middle of *Jeopardy!* I knew better than to complain, even though it was my favorite show. There's something so encouraging about it, the way it makes you believe America's populated by these brilliant ordinary people, postal workers and data entry operators and office managers whose heads are somehow crammed full of information about Greek Mythology, Chinese History, and Voyages of Discovery. It cheered me up every night.

Mom took a deep breath but forgot to release it. Her eyes were shadowy with fatigue and her cheeks looked rubbery. It was almost like Dad had packed her youth in a cardboard box and lugged it off to that ugly little townhouse by the highway.

"Tammy," she said, "I'm worried about us."

I'd planned on going into a trance of agreement—total nodding mode—but her pronoun threw me off balance.

"Us?" I said.

"We're not a family anymore. We're all at each

other's throats. Your father and me. Now you and Paul. I can't believe we've come to this."

She hadn't really asked a question, so I figured it was okay to keep my mouth shut.

"Why are you doing it?" she asked. "Are you angry with me?"

"Doing what?"

Her shoulders slumped. She finally let go of that breath.

"Tammy, don't make this harder than it is."

"I'm not. I didn't understand the question."

"Okay," she said, discharging her annoyance in a quick sidelong glance. "Let me put it this way. Why are you running against your brother?"

"I'm not running *against* him. I'm just running. Why can't people understand that?"

She shut her eyes, pinching at her forehead with two fingers like it was made of clay. She looked exhausted.

"Before you know it, honey, Paul's going to be leaving for college. And then you're going to leave, too. Do you see what I'm saying?"

I nodded, though it seemed to me we'd gotten a little off track.

"I'm going to be alone," she said, in a voice so sad and puny it made me want to cry.

I reached for her hand, the one that still had the wedding ring on it, and gave it a squeeze.

"Don't worry, Mom. You'll be okay."

"Be nice to your brother," she told me. "He's the only one you've got."

She tucked a piece of hair behind my ear with a melancholy sigh, then got up and trudged back to the kitchen. I didn't even miss Final Jeopardy.

After that I had three full days to watch soap operas, write in my journal, and explore the empty house. My brother, I discovered, kept his condoms in a hollowed-out paperback dictionary secured by a red rubber band. There were five of them, lubricated Trojans in blue foil pouches. For about an hour after finding them I felt sick to my stomach. Then I had this fantasy of pricking one of them with a needle, making this tiny imperceptible hole. It pleased me to imagine Lisa waddling through the halls of Winwood, pregnant with the President's baby. I wondered how Mr. Hendricks would feel about that.

The second afternoon I read one of those Sweet Valley High books I used to love so much. All through seventh grade I'd been captivated by the Wakefield twins and their many friends, perky California girls and hunky, well-to-do boys who cruised in fancy cars, kissed on the beach, and confronted the difficult dilemmas of growing up with dignity and courage.

It seemed like a total dreamworld to me now that I was in high school myself. I could only imagine Elizabeth Wakefield's shock—she was the good twin, the one I had the crush on—if she were to spend a week or two in the real world. She'd go back to Sweet Valley with cramps, a filthy mouth, and a bad case of acne. Not even her sister would recognize her.

PAUL WARREN

A PART OF ME—one I never expressed to anyone—thought it might be better if Tammy won the election. She needed the boost a lot more than I did.

If you're a guy who's good at sports, your social life just sort of falls into place. I never had to search too hard for girlfriends, people to hang out with, or places to go on Saturday night.

It wasn't like that for Tammy. She wasn't too popular or outgoing to begin with, and hadn't found any new friends to replace Lisa. Night after night she hung around the house with Mom, sulking in front of the TV. The phone never rang for either of them.

As far as I knew, my little sister never had a boyfriend, had never even been kissed. I thought about this a lot when I was with Lisa, who turned out to be so much wilder than you would have imagined from looking at her. It made me wonder if Tammy was the same way, if she had a secret life I was just too dense to notice.

One night, after Lisa and I had experimented for the first time with oral sex, I asked her point-blank: "Is Tammy like you?"

The question startled her.

"What's that supposed to mean?"

"Does she do stuff like this?"

Lisa seemed uncomfortable.

"Stuff like what?"

"Like we just did."

We were sprawled out on her bedroom floor, naked except for T-shirts, the summer seashore taste of her still faintly on my lips. I'd been scared to do it at first, but now I was exhilarated, eager to try again. Her mother was at a singles' meeting, and wouldn't be home for at least another hour.

"Why are you asking me?"

"I'm just trying to figure out if she's as innocent as she looks. I thought you might know."

Lisa didn't answer. I kissed the pale oval scar on her right knee. Aside from that small, eye-shaped blemish, her body was perfect, unmarked, as lean and smooth as a little girl's, except for the subtle curves of her hips and the unexpected fullness of her ass. She leaned back on both elbows and watched my tongue wander up her quadricep. Her legs were strong and sculpted from running, and she seemed to like having them licked.

"Oh," she said, very softly.

It's funny about sex. Once you start, you can't re-member how you got along without it. What did you think about? How did you fill up your day? You find yourself wondering why you'd even *want* to be Presi-dent, when you already have this wonderful way of spending your time.

TAMMY WARREN

IT WAS SPOOKY to go back to school after my suspen-sion and see these unreal color posters of Paul plastered all over the place, sporting these dopey slogans like "Paul Power" and "We Need Him." Every time I turned a cor-ner my big brother was watching me, gazing down from the walls and bulletin boards like some kind of puzzled blond god.

I knew from a single glance that Lisa had done the artwork. She liked drawing with pastels and had once done a portrait of me standing by a window, bathed in morning light, watching leaves fall from a golden tree. When she felt like it, she knew how to flatter a person.

Tracy had even more posters than Paul did. They were red, white, and blue, and looked suspiciously pro-fessional, like the signs you see taped to telephone poles during real elections. "Pick Flick," advised one of them. "Tracy for Prez," proclaimed another.

I didn't plan on doing any campaigning. I figured I could just coast into the election and lose gracefully, the one candidate who'd had the guts to tell the truth and had been punished for her honesty. It seemed like a decent way to go down in history.

The three days at home had been good for me. I'd discovered this great yoga program on cable, and had learned how to meditate along with the host, the calmest, most sweet-voiced woman in the universe. She told me to imagine my heart as a big red valentine throbbing in my chest, and advised me to release all the negativity I'd allowed to build up inside it. So I did. I let go of my jealousy and anger and need to hurt the people who'd hurt me. Once I did that, there wasn't much reason left for me to even want to be President.

But a funny thing happened that morning when I got back to school. Kids I didn't even know came up and shook my hand, telling me what a cool speech I'd made and how they were definitely going to vote for me. A girl in a wheelchair gave me a thumbs-up. This greasy-haired sophomore arsonist told me I kicked ass. Some of the nicer teachers flashed me sly, private smiles. Mr. Herrera even winked. These two weird freshman guys—bug-eyed Nintendo geeks—invited me to a party they insisted was going to be totally wild.

It was just like the yoga lady said: Expel the negative, and the positive will come rushing in to fill the void.

MR. M.

IT WAS THE MOST interesting election I'd seen in my nine years at Winwood. There was a buzz in the hallways, an excitement that couldn't be accounted for solely by the novelty of sibling competition. There was just this sense throughout the whole school that for once we had an election that offered a real choice.

Paul was running as a visual image—the Student as Hero. Idealized in pastel colors, he presided over our corridors like some kind of benevolent, otherworldly spirit. There was something at once comforting and unnerving about those portraits; you'd see people standing in front of them for improbable lengths of time, studying them like paintings in a museum.

Tracy had taken the opposite tack. She seemed to be running not as a student, but as a professional politician. Simple as they were—plain red letters on blue cardboard, the *i* in her last name dotted with a bold white star—her posters had clearly been designed by a graphic artist and manufactured by a printer at no small expense. You got the feeling she was running for State Legislature.

Tammy's posters weren't posters at all, just cryptic messages scribbled on notebook paper, affixed to unlikely surfaces—a file cabinet, the seat of a chair, the inside of a bathroom stall.

"Vote for Tammy," they might say. "She's inexperienced and kind of lazy."

Or: "Election? What Election?"

Or: "Go Ahead. Make the Stupid Choice."

It got to be a little game. You'd walk into a classroom and see the words "Why Not?" scrawled across an otherwise empty blackboard. You'd unscroll your fold-down map of the world and not be surprised to find a pink index card taped to the Horn of Africa, bearing the following statistic: "Two out of three coffee drinkers prefer Tammy to fresh-brewed." If you saw a wad of paper on the floor, you'd bend down and uncrumple it, just in case.

6

PAUL WARREN

THE BRUNCH WAS my father's idea. He'd been feeling isolated and thought it would be good for all of us
to get together on neutral ground to celebrate Tammy's
birthday.

"We're still a family," he reminded me. "Whatever
happens, we can't let ourselves forget that."

He told me this in the bedroom / living room of his
small, mostly unfurnished apartment in Rock Hill Gar-
dens, an ugly complex overlooking the Parkway. I'd
stopped in on my way home from Lisa's, as I often did, to
watch the ten o'clock news with him on the tiny portable
TV Mom used to keep on the kitchen counter.

We'd grown a lot closer since the separation. At
home he'd been kind of distant, not really interested in
talking about anything but sports. Here, though, maybe

out of guilt or loneliness, he seemed to feel a power-ful urge to explain himself, to make me understand the circumstances that had driven him out of our big, comfortable house into this garage-sized studio.

This new phase of our relationship had begun the day I helped him move, against my will and at my mother's insistence. For two hours we lugged boxes and suitcases and household furnishings from the parking lot to the apartment, communicating in our everyday language of grunts and gestures, with a few words tossed in to avoid confusion. We were grappling with the dead weight of his new mattress when he looked at me, his face pink with effort, and said something totally unex-pected.

"No one knows what love is," he told me. "If some-one says they do, they're full of shit."

I didn't reply. We steered the mattress through the doorway, letting it fall with a muffled *whump* to the carpeted floor.

"Some people think it's a plant you have to water," he went on, checking to see if I was paying attention. "I believe your mother subscribes to this metaphor." He hesitated. "You know what a metaphor is, right?"

"Yeah," I said, a little surprised to hear a word like that coming out of his mouth.

"Most people use metaphors to talk about love and that's why they get it wrong. It's physical, Paul. It's a feeling you carry around in your body. I'd lost that with your mother."

I stared down at my sneakers, as though trying to see through them to the clenched toes inside. It didn't seem possible that he was telling me this, any more than it seemed possible that he had actually traded Mom for Mrs. Stiller. Mom was slender and quiet, a pretty, thoughtful woman with a soft laugh. And Mrs. Stiller...

"She's fat." I just blurted it out. My father's girl-friend was a loud fat woman who sold real estate.

He nodded. "I thought I'd be disgusted by her body, but I wasn't." His eyes grew slitlike as he gnawed on a thumbnail. "I was moved, Paul. By the sight of her."

I stood there, trying to breathe. My lungs didn't seem to be working right.

"She's gross," I said. "She's a fat fucking pig."

He took a step in my direction. I wanted to make him mad, but it wasn't working. This crooked little smile started to take shape on his face.

"You know what? She doesn't eat any more than you or me. She's just heavy. There's nothing she can do about it."

He reported this to me as though it were some marvelous fact, something I'd want to share with my friends.

"Heavy?" I said. "She's a fucking sumo wrestler."

I tried to say something else about what a tub of

fucking lard she was, but I was too busy choking back
sobs. My father moved closer, laying one hand on top
of my shoulder. He put his arm around me and pulled
me against his chest. He smelled the way he had the
last time I'd hugged him, way back in third or second
grade.

TAMMY WARREN

I HADN'T GONE out in a long time, and Mom was all
excited, like it was prom night or something. She super-
vised my hair and kept trying to get me to change into a
dress.

"Mom," I said. "Would you get real? These guys
play Nintendo like nineteen hours a day. I'll be
overdressed if my socks match."

"Are they cute?"

"Cute?" I clutched my head. "These guys sleep in
their clothes, Mom."

She waved her hands in surrender.

"All right, all right. Forget I even asked." She started
backing out of the room, but stopped in the doorway to
offer one last piece of advice. "Believe me, honey. A little
lipstick never hurt anyone."

So I put on some lipstick, just to make her happy. It
didn't look bad, though I might've cared a little more if

there'd been someone in the world I wanted to kiss who had the slightest desire to kiss me back.

The party was across town, and Mom had enlisted Paul to drop me off on his way to Lisa's and pick me up on the way home. He was waiting in the living room with his coat on, impatiently tapping his foot. He jumped up when he saw me, and told me I looked great. Being in love had turned him into a much nicer person.

"Doesn't she?" Mom smiled, brand-new wrinkles tugging at the corners of her eyes and mouth. "Your baby sister's growing up."

She kissed us goodbye and stood alone beneath the porch light, waving as we backed out of the driveway.

"Poor Mom," I said.

Paul nodded, frowning as he wiggled the gearshift. He'd only been driving for a couple of months.

"I wish she'd get out more," he said. "Meet some new people. Lisa's mom belongs to a singles' group. She's out on a date tonight."

"Really?" I tried not to sound too interested. "What are you guys doing?"

He shrugged. "Hang out. Maybe watch some TV."

We drove in silence for a few minutes, long enough for me to realize that it was the first time we'd ever been alone in a car. It was amazing in a quiet way, the kind of moment we couldn't have even imagined as little kids, pinching and tickling each other in the backseat. On long drives I used to fall asleep with my head in his lap. Sometimes, out of the blue like that, even when I was mad at him, I'd suddenly remember that Paul was my brother and I loved him. He looked at me, almost like he could read my mind.

"You know that brunch tomorrow?"

"Yeah?"

"You mind if I bring Lisa?"

The speedometer glowed on the dashboard, a ring of luminous green.

"Do what you want."

We turned down Grove and stopped in front of number 71. I unbuckled my seat belt and reached for the door handle.

"Hey," he said. "Whatever happened with you two anyway?"

"Why don't you ask her?"

"I do. She never answers."

MR. M.

FOR SIX OR SEVEN MONTHS Diane and I had been trying to get pregnant, dancing to the joyless tune of calendar and thermometer. On doctor's orders, I traded in my briefs for boxers, which I found uncomfortable, and we restricted ourselves to the sexual positions most likely to facilitate conception (not that we'd been that wild to begin with). When it was over, Diane lay perfectly still for ten minutes, hugging her knees to her chest as she visualized the hoped-for collision between sperm and egg.

All that hard work took its toll. Despite my wife's misgivings, I found it increasingly difficult to perform on demand for several consecutive nights without the aid and inspiration of dirty magazines. It wasn't that Diane objected to pornography on feminist grounds; she just disliked comparing herself to the women in the pictures, whose bodies seemed to her so effortlessly and inhumanly beautiful. After a few inconclusive fights, we struck a tacit bargain, whereby I was allowed to consult my magazines as long as she could pretend not to know about it. Practically speaking, this meant that I spent a lot of time in the bathroom right before sex, trying to coax myself into the right frame of mind.

And sometimes even that wasn't enough. After losing my erection on a couple of occasions, I took the advice of a TV sexologist and began fantasizing about women other than my wife. One night it would be Ellen DiNardo, the sexy new art teacher, and the next it would be Michelle Pfeiffer, or Mary Tyler Moore in her incarnation as Laura Petrie.

One night, shortly after the Candidate Assembly, as Diane impassively spread her legs, I closed my eyes and pretended she was Tracy Flick. The fantasy was vivid and explosive; we were fucking without tenderness beneath the bleachers during an important football game, the noise of the crowd barely muffling our animal grunts and exchanges of foul language. Skirt pulled up, tights yanked down, she thrashed her head from side to side on the confetti-speckled pavement, arching her hips to meet my powerful thrusts. I came with a series of violent shudders that racked my whole body. I was barely finished when Diane shoved me off of her, drawing her knees to her chest as the doctor had instructed. I rolled onto my back, raggedly panting, my skin filmy with sweat. Diane turned her head and studied me with what I took to be mild interest.

"Jim," she said, "would you turn on Jay Leno?"

TAMMY WARREN

A PRETTY GIRL I'd never seen before answered the door and took my coat.

"I'm Dana," she said. "Jason's my stepbrother."

Jason Caputo and Lance Breezey, the Nintendo geeks, were in the living room, drinking beer and playing Super Mario Brothers. It didn't seem like much of a party.

"Am I early?"

Lance shook his head, working the controls with furious concentration. All sorts of annoying sounds emerged from the TV as the little cartoon men jumped and shot fireballs.

"You're right on time," he assured me.

"Where's everyone else?"

Jason looked at me for the first time since I'd arrived, his excited face opening into a slow, crazy-eyed smile. His hair was a mess of cowlicks, his pink and green rugby shirt too tight even for his painfully thin body. He looked like he'd just rolled out of bed after a long illness.

"You *are* everyone else," he told me. "We wanted to keep things intimate."

I followed Dana into the kitchen, surprised that a dork like Jason could even have a stepsister as cool as her, a girl you wouldn't have been surprised to see dancing on MTV, her body loose, her face a mask of sultry boredom. She wore baggy overalls and a tight, striped jersey that didn't reach her navel. Her dark straight hair fell at a severe angle across one eye.

"I'm glad you came," she said, grimacing as she twisted the cap off a beer bottle. "Those two drive me crazy after a while."

"Where do you go to school?" I asked.

She handed me the beer. "Immaculate Mary."

"Do you like it?"

"It's okay. At least we don't have to go through the

bullshit with the makeup and clothes every day. You can show up looking like a wreck and nobody even cares."

I took a tiny sip of beer, holding my breath so I didn't have to taste it.

"You wear uniforms?"

"Yeah." She pushed the hair out of her face, momentarily exposing a large shapeless birthmark spreading from her cheekbone to her forehead. It was amazing how thoroughly it was concealed by her haircut. "Blue knee socks, gray skirts, white blouses. Five days a week. And saddle shoes."

"No overalls," I said, thinking again how cool she looked, and how exotic with that secret birthmark.

"Nope." She reached into one of her many pockets and pulled out a pack of cigarettes. "Want one?"

"Sure."

We had to go out on the deck because of Jason's allergies. I lit my cigarette off hers and smoked it in tiny puffs that felt like razors going down my throat. Dana was even clumsier than I was, choking on every other drag.

"I only smoke at parties," I said, admiring the sophistication of the remark.

"Same here," she said. "Only when I drink."

The night was chilly, but I didn't mind. I'd forgotten how good it felt to get out of the house, to escape into something new.

"I guess I should warn you," she said. "Jason's got this really big crush on you."

"On me?" I laughed too loud, as if this were the most ridiculous thing I'd ever heard.

She nodded gravely. "He talks about you all the time."

Dana flicked her cigarette into the yard. I did the same, relieved to get rid of it. They landed just a couple of inches apart in the grass, burning through the darkness like two orange stars.

MR. M.

ANOTHER WOMAN I fantasized about was Sherry Dexter, but with her I was slow and careful, a healer of sorrows. It was especially exciting for me because we spent so much time together in real life.

Diane and I drove to her house almost every night and stayed until ten or eleven, doing double duty as friends and babysitters, giving Sherry a chance to take a shower, eat a meal in peace, maybe run a quick errand without having to worry about Darren. She said it was heaven to go to the supermarket by herself; she felt so streamlined and free gliding up and down the aisles without a baby in tow, so much like a real person.

It was marvelous to watch the transformation she

underwent in our presence. She answered the door in a food-stained sweatsuit, hair pulled back any which way, her face pasty and frazzled. After a few minutes of small talk she escaped upstairs for a shower that sometimes lasted as long as a half hour. I could imagine the luxury of it, the steam and privacy, the chance to be alone in her own body for the first time all day without worries or distractions.

She was a different person when she came back down. Her wet hair was loose, freshly combed, her skin rosy. The smell of shampoo clung to her like a warm aura. Sometimes she got dressed, but I preferred the nights when she rejoined us in her crimson terry cloth robe, a garment that had figured prominently in a couple of my fantasies.

A strange intimacy seemed to have sprouted up between us that spring, as if she'd somehow gotten wind of the things we did together in my head and wanted me to know that she approved. She smiled at me on the flimsiest of pretexts, spoke my name as if it belonged to another Jim, a witty, fascinating man whose company brought her immense pleasure.

If Diane noticed, it didn't seem to bother her; she only had eyes for Darren. As soon as we arrived, her eyes lit up with fresh wonder at the sight of his scrunched and quizzical face, so eerily reminiscent of Jack's. For the next hour or two, until Darren grew cranky with exhaustion, they played together on the floor — sorting shapes, reading nursery rhymes, building the same four-block tower over and over again — leaving Sherry and me free to continue our flirtation at a slightly higher altitude, safe in the knowledge that it couldn't really go anywhere.

One night, though, about a week before the election, Sherry came down from her shower dressed to go out. On what seemed like the spur of the moment, she invited Diane to drive with her to the mall.

"I need to pick up a housewarming gift for my sister," she said. "I hate to drive all that way by myself."

Diane didn't answer right away. She was kneeling on the floor, adding the last alphabet block to a precarious tower as Darren looked on, gleefully awaiting her permission to demolish it.

"Take Jim," she said offhandedly. "I'm happy right here."

Sherry and I exchanged a swift glance of collusion and alarm. The color deepened in her cheeks and throat.

"Oh no," she said. "I'm sure he'd be bored to death."

"Not at all," I told her. "I'm happy to be your escort."

DANA HAD A VCR in her bedroom and her own copy of *Truth or Dare*. We sat on her bed in the flickering darkness beneath a huge poster of Jason Priestley, watching in almost religious silence. Whenever a song came on we jumped off the bed and started dancing around like maniacs.

Dana did a great Madonna imitation. She knew most of the routines pretty much by heart, except for the really complicated parts, and didn't seem embarrassed about running her hands up and down her body.

"Don't worry," she told me. "I won't do the masturbation scene."

The first time I saw *Truth or Dare* was in a movie theater, and I was totally hypnotized by Madonna. She was all I remembered: Madonna at her mother's grave, Madonna putting that bottle in her mouth, Madonna sad and lonely in a beautiful hotel room. It was like she gave off this exclusive brightness, blinding you to anyone and anything that wasn't her.

On the smaller screen she was less dazzling, more like a human being. I found myself paying closer attention to the other people in the movie — the dancers, the chubby makeup girl, the childhood friend who asks Madonna to be her baby's godmother. I tried to imagine what it would be like to be a member of her family, how hard it would be to keep your spirits up, to wake up in the morning and actually believe you have a life worth living.

One of her brothers worked for her, and one had just gotten out of rehab. Her father seemed both awed and frightened by who she was and what she did in front of thousands of people. The father's wife didn't like Madonna very much. It must have been strange for her, marrying a completely ordinary man whose daughter turns out to be the most famous person in the world.

I thought about my own father, and how satisfying it would be to bring him and Mrs. Stiller to one of my concerts, then invite them back to my dressing room afterward so they could get a close-up glimpse of what a huge star I was. I also thought about Paul, how I'd spent so much time resenting him for being so handsome and clueless and successful, when he was really just another nobody. Madonna wouldn't have given him the time of day.

"I can't believe she does this with her dad in the audience," Dana marveled. "It's so weird."

Madonna was writhing on the bed, pretending to give herself an orgasm. My breath quickened as I watched, my blood beginning to hum. Dana and I were a couple of inches apart. We didn't look at each other or move a muscle. We just sat wide-eyed, staring straight ahead until it was over.

MR. M.

SHERRY SMILED at me as we pulled away from the curb.

"Well," she said. "Here we are."

"Yup," I replied. "Here we are."

The humid smell of her shampoo wafted through the car like a mysterious tropical breeze. I breathed deeply, taking as much of it as I could into my lungs.

"It's been a long time since I've been out with a man," she told me.

"Don't worry. I'll behave myself."

She laughed merrily.

"I know," she said. "That's what worries me."

TAMMY WARREN

THE TAPE WAS rewinding when Lance and Jason pushed open the door and asked if we wanted to play spin the bottle.

"No way," said Dana. "There aren't enough of us."

"Sure there are," said Jason.

"Forget it," said Dana. "I'm not kissing you."

"You don't have to," he assured her. "I can kiss Tammy. And both of you can kiss Lance."

Lance snickered. "And you two can kiss each other."

I had the weirdest feeling then, like it might really happen. Dana stood there, shaking her head.

"You guys are pathetic," she said.

MR. M.

SHERRY BOUGHT a toaster. I behaved myself. Both of us seemed relieved as we slipped back into the car, as if we'd passed some sort of test.

"Thanks," she told me. "I appreciate the company."

"No problem."

"You guys are great friends. I don't know what I'd do without you."

If we'd made it home on that note, everything would have been okay. But fate conspired against us. We happened to catch a red light just outside the Benedict Motel, one of those hourly-rate places that exist solely to provide a haven for illicit sex. Nine o'clock on Thursday night and the parking lot was almost completely full. I'm still not sure what possessed me to open my mouth.

"Should I pull in?"

She didn't laugh or feign shock. Her gaze was level, her voice tight and serious.

"Don't ask me again," she said. "Not unless you really want an answer."

7

TRACY FLICK

WINWOOD'S A RICH TOWN, but not everyone who lives here is rich. Since my parents split up six years ago, my mother's supported us on the money she makes as a legal secretary. My father helps out, but not as much or as often as he should (he's got a new wife now, and a two year-old son). If it weren't for loans and scholarships, you can bet I wouldn't be going to an expensive school like Georgetown.

It's not like we're poor. It's just that we've learned to do without a lot of things that most people around here take for granted—nice vacations, new cars, expensive clothes, even cable TV. The house we live in is a big Victorian on Maple Street, one of the prettiest blocks in town. We rent the whole second floor for only five hundred a month, about half the going rate. Winwood's a commuter town, and nice apartments don't come cheap.

"Our landlord's a saint," my mother tells people every chance she gets. "If it weren't for him, we'd probably be living on the street."

LISA FLANAGAN

"IT'S OKAY with Tammy," he'd assured me. "She says it's no big deal."

But it wasn't okay with Tammy. We were sharing the backseat and she didn't even look at me when I climbed in and wished her a happy birthday. She just kept staring out the window in the wrong direction, as if fascinated by the gray house across the street.

Mrs. Warren turned in the passenger seat, trying to smooth over the awkwardness. She looked older than I remembered, and her smile was tense, an effort of will.

"Oh Lisa," she said. "It's so nice to see you again."

"It's nice to see you too, Mrs. Warren."

It was weird how stiff and artificial we sounded. Only a year ago Mrs. Warren and I had been able to giggle and gossip like girlfriends. But so much had changed since then that our shared past seemed to have happened to other people, or not to have happened at all.

That went double for me and Tammy. It didn't seem possible that we'd ever held hands at the movies or kissed until we were dizzy. If we'd been on speaking terms, I might've told her that I'd come to think of sex as this long dark tunnel that turns friends into strangers, strangers into friends.

TRACY FLICK

OUR LANDLORD IS Joe Delvecchio, chief of the maintenance crew at Winwood High. He's a familiar figure around the school, wandering the halls with a bottle of Windex or a screwdriver in his hand, whistling some dopey tune from the fifties.

Janitors fall into a gray area at school. They're adults, but they don't really count. They can't discipline you or give you bad grades. They shuffle around in their blue uniforms, condemned to mop floors, erase graffiti, clean bathrooms, and suffer abuse at the hands of teenagers. It's almost like they're put there as a warning, to remind you of what might happen if you don't pay attention in class or do your homework.

Joe's different, though; he's a janitor by choice rather than necessity. He used to be a cop, but he retired with half pay after hurting his back in a scuffle with a shoplifter. He hated sitting around and eventually escaped his boredom by signing on as janitor and all-around handyman at the high school. He says it keeps him young.

At home, Joe and I are friends. I help him shovel the snow and take care of the lawn; he and his wife do all kinds of favors for my mother and me. At school, though, we don't have a lot of contact. We'll smile and say hello, but that's about it. Watching us in the hall, you wouldn't know that we exchange Christmas gifts, or that he likes to call me "princess."

TAMMY WARREN

DAD WAS SITTING alone at a big round table, pretending to read the menu, looking for all the world like the sad thing he was—a family man who had somehow misplaced his family. My mother clutched my arm.

"Help me get through this," she whispered.

He'd grown a beard since I'd last seen him. It was neatly trimmed, flecked with gray, surprisingly distinguished. You might have thought he was a professor or a movie director instead of a man who sold unbreakable windows to stores in bad neighborhoods.

Mom flinched at his lame kiss. He helped her into

her chair, then turned to me with this expression of bogus wonder, like he was too moved by the sight of me even to speak.

"The name's Tammy," I told him. "I'm your daughter."

That wiped the cornball look off his face. He didn't get mad, though.

"Oh yeah," he said, smiling like an actual human being. "I thought you looked familiar."

He and Paul hugged like brothers, clapping each other three times on the back before letting go. He greeted Lisa with one of his deeply sincere, two-handed Dale Carnegie handshakes.

"Ms. Flanagan," he said. "Don't you look lovely today."

And she did, too. She was wearing a short yellow skirt with black tights and a stretchy black top, and you couldn't help but notice how sleek and graceful she was. It hurt me just to look at her.

TRACY FLICK

IT WAS the Sunday before the election. Joe was right where I expected him to be, in the driveway, tinkering with the engine of his Cadillac. It was a penny-colored Fleetwood with white leather seats, not the kind of car you'd expect a janitor to drive. He washed it every week and changed the oil like clockwork, every three months.

"Joe," I said, "can I ask you a humongous favor?"

"Sure, princess."

"I forgot my math book in my locker."

He straightened up, wiping his greasy hands on an old dish towel. He didn't look too happy.

"Yeah?"

"We've got a big test tomorrow."

He cocked one eyebrow a fraction of an inch, then nodded very slowly to let me know his patience was beginning to wear thin. This was the third weekend in a row I'd supposedly forgotten something in my locker.

"Okay," he said. "I've got to stop in for a minute anyway. How's two?"

"Two's great."

I'm not sure why I went through the charade with the math book. Joe knew exactly what I was up to. At two o'clock I met him in the driveway with a box of campaign posters in my arms and a tape dispenser sticking out of my jacket pocket.

PAUL WARREN

"SO TELL ME," said Dad. "Who's gonna win this election?"

Lisa shot me a surprised glance, her pretty eyes widening with alarm. Tammy stared blankly at her pancakes. Mom twisted her head, apparently searching for our waitress. Dad pressed on.

"What's the matter? We're all intelligent people. Doesn't anyone have an opinion?"

The whole brunch had gone like that, Dad playing teacher, the rest of us fumbling for answers. Mom was stiff and tongue-tied, Tammy sullen, Lisa polite. I'd done my best to keep the conversation afloat, but I was starting to lose heart.

"I'm a lifelong Republican," he went on, "but I'm actually thinking about pulling the lever for Jerry Brown."

The sense of relief around the table was immediate and conspicuous.

"Jerry Brown?" Mom scoffed. "You've got to be kidding."

"I'm serious," he insisted. "This country's corrupt from top to bottom, and Brown's the only one with the guts to say so."

"Perot's saying it too," Lisa reminded them.

"He's nuttier than Brown," Mom observed. "The ears on that man."

"What about Clinton?" I asked. "He's pretty interesting."

"Ugh." Dad looked disgusted. "That guy. He could stand out in the rain all day and not get wet."

"I'm surprised," said Mom. "I had you pegged for a Clinton man."

"Me?" he said. "What gave you that idea?"

TRACY FLICK

THE SCHOOL ALWAYS seemed so big with no one around, so clean and silent and forgotten. Every noise I made—every squeak of my sneakers, every rip of tape and rustle of paper—echoed spookily in that vast emptiness.

Joe had disappeared into his closet of an office, leaving me to decorate the hallways in perfect solitude. It was easier to do this work in private, invisibly, to not be caught in the embarrassing but necessary task of self-promotion. I fixed my posters to every fifth locker, pleased by the effect of my name stretching rhythmically down the endless corridor—*Tracy Flick, Tracy Flick, Tracy Flick*—like the school itself was whispering its true preference. I liked the idea of everyone walking in on Monday morning, fresh and well rested, to be greeted by my bright new message.

I'm not sure why, but being alone in the building always made me think of Jack. Only the good parts came back to me, the long talks and stolen kisses, the adventure of our sneaking around, the way the building seemed to conspire with our secret. There was always an empty room to duck into, another dark corner waiting to hide us from the world. The school was our playground and refuge. As soon as we stepped outside its boundaries, the rules changed and everyone got hurt.

Room 17 used to be his classroom. I pressed my nose to the window of the door, fogging the glass with my warm breath. I wanted to see him leaning back in his chair, both hands behind his head. I wanted to see myself sitting a few feet away, telling him about this great idea I'd had for *The Watchdog*.

"Tracy," he'd say. "Slow down. One word at a time."

But there was no sign of him in the empty room, no posters of Michael Jordan and Ernest Hemingway, no bowling pin on top of the file cabinet, no "Word of the Day" calendar anchoring the blotter of his tiny desk. Miss Benson had changed everything.

I still get letters from Jack. He says he's not mad at me, that he only got what he deserved. He tells me about his job at the hardware store, and about the novel he's thinking about trying to write. He wants to know if I'm seeing anyone.

PAUL WARREN

"THIS IS GOOD CAKE," said Mom.

"Sure is," agreed Dad.

Lisa and I concurred. We all stared at Tammy, waiting for her to make it unanimous. She broke off a tiny piece with her fork, chewed it thoughtfully, then swallowed.

"I want to go to Catholic school," she announced.

"Excuse me?" said Mom.

"I said I want to transfer to Catholic school. Immaculate Mary."

She sounded serious. Dad scratched his beard.

"Why would you want to do that?"

"I need a change."

Mom looked puzzled.

"Honey, we're not Catholic."

Tammy rolled her eyes. She took another bite of cake and surveyed the table.

"That's all girls," I reminded her.

"I know."

"You have to wear uniforms," Lisa muttered.

"I know." Tammy smiled. "Don't you think I'd look cute?"

TRACY FLICK

ABOUT HALFWAY THROUGH, I ran into an obstacle. One of Paul's ridiculous posters was taped to a locker that I needed to use.

The locker belonged to his girlfriend, Lisa Flanagan. I guess I could've skipped it, but I didn't want to break the rhythm. I wanted to cover the whole school, every fifth locker.

The poster smirked at me, and something about it made me angry. Maybe it was Paul's sweet handsome face, or maybe it was that stupid slogan: WE NEED HIM. Maybe it was the way he and Lisa kissed in front of everyone, like they were getting nourishment from each other's tongues. Really, though, it was because in spite of everything—in spite of his pathetic speech and my superior experience with student government and his sister's presence in the race—he was probably going to win. Not because he deserved it, but simply because he was Paul Warren.

Can you imagine if I'd lined the hallways with pictures of my face? People would have laughed me out of the school.

"What a bitch!" they'd say. "Who does she think she is?"

I didn't really think about it. I just looked down and saw the poster in my hands, ripped into two unequal pieces.

8

MR. M.

I GOT IN LATE the Monday before the election, the one morning of the year Walt Hendricks needed to see me first thing. He'd worked himself into a minor frenzy waiting for me to show up.

"Goddammit Jim, where the hell were you? We've got ourselves a fucking problem."

"What's that?"

Walt took a sip of coffee and grimaced like it was vinegar. His green and yellow plaid sportcoat was not available in any store.

"It's this election of yours. What's-her-name was just in here sobbing. God, I hate that shit."

"What's-her-name?"

"You know. The flat-chested one. Paul's girlfriend."

"Lisa Flanagan."

"That's it." Walt's face grew mournful as he cupped his flabby pectorals. "Flat as a board, Jim."

"She was crying?"

He twisted the top off a bottle of Tylenol, shook three extra-strength Caplets into his palm, and swallowed them without the aid of liquid.

"Hope they're laced with cyanide," he muttered. "Put me out of my misery."

"What was she crying about?"

His hands turned in vague spirals around his ears, as if the whole thing were too complicated for words.

"Something about Paul's posters. She came in this morning and they were gone. Someone ripped them off the walls."

The phone rang on his desk. He lifted the receiver, then slammed it back down in its cradle.

"See?" he told me. "This is what I do with my fucking life. I'm barely in here two minutes and already I have to suspend someone. What's with these kids anyway? Nobody used to rip posters off the walls."

"So what do you want me to do?"

He cocked his head and stared at me as though I were a complete imbecile.

"Get to the bottom of it. Tell me who I have to discipline. What's-her-name thinks it was Flick, but I wouldn't be surprised if it was Paul's little bitch of a sister."

TRACY FLICK

OKAY, so I lost my head and ripped a couple of posters. From the way people reacted, you would have thought I'd murdered Paul Warren and stuffed the dismembered pieces of his body into my locker.

Mr. M. called me out of study hall for a one-on-one interrogation in his classroom. I'm surprised he didn't have a tape recorder and one of those blinding spotlights shining on my face.

"I guess you know why you're here."

"Aren't you supposed to read me my rights?"

"Very funny." He made a few preliminary squiggles on a piece of scratch paper, then looked up. "Did you do it?"

In a perfect world, I could've just confessed: *Yes, I ripped the first one by accident and it felt so good that I decided to rip the rest. It was stupid and I'm sorry.* But it wasn't a perfect world, and I wasn't about to get myself suspended the day before the election.

"Are you accusing me?"

He closed his eyes and sat there for a few seconds without speaking, like he'd forgotten all about me. Mr. M. wasn't as cute as Jack, but he had nice eyelashes and thick curly hair.

"No one is accusing you of anything, Tracy. I'm just asking you a simple question."

"Well, the answer is no."

His smile was patronizing, as if he'd fully expected me to lie.

"Frankly," he said, "I find that hard to believe."

"Why?"

"Because it looks like the posters were defaced over the weekend. That means the perpetrator had to have access to the building on Saturday or Sunday."

My face got hot. Mr. M. was a friend of Jack's, and I had this uncomfortable feeling he knew everything about me.

"How would I get in on the weekend?"

He shrugged like Columbo. "Who knows, Tracy. Maybe it wasn't you. Maybe it was one of the janitors. I guess I could call them in for questioning."

My stomach hurt and I started to get scared. I tried to imagine what my mother might do in this situation.

"Can I make a phone call?"

"Why?"

"I need to talk to my lawyer."

That startled him. He gave me a look like I was from another planet.

"Your *lawyer?*"

"My mother's a legal secretary. Her boss handles all our litigation."

"Whoa, Tracy." Mr. M. signaled for a time-out. "You're getting a little ahead of yourself."

I knew an advantage when I saw one. I made my voice as indignant as possible.

"Well, I'm not about to sit here and be accused of something I didn't do."

He shook his head, studying me with a deep, unspoken disgust. I should have realized then that he was prepared to hurt me if he thought he could get away with it.

"Get the hell out of here," he said. "You're giving me a headache."

MR. M.

NONE OF IT was real to me, not Walt's ravings or Paul's vanished posters, not Tracy's laughable threats of legal action. The only thing that was real to me was Sherry Dexter and the line we'd crossed that morning in her living room.

I'd stopped by her house on the way to school, supposedly to drop off this John Grisham novel she'd been bugging me about. I expected her to be dressed for work, but she answered the door in a blue oxford shirt of Jack's and nothing else, an outfit I thought women only wore in TV commercials. Her smile was shy and inviting.

I handed her the book. She glanced at the cover, then laughed and tossed it over her shoulder. In a single fluid motion she stepped into my arms and kicked the door shut with her bare foot. Her body was warm through the soft cotton, sweeter than I'd dreamed. I felt no guilt, only a joy so pure it hurt.

"This is wrong," she said, reaching for my belt buckle.

"Awful," I agreed, peering over her shoulder to check my watch. "Things are going to get complicated."

We made love right there on the floor, surrounded by the colorful clutter of Darren's toys. It wasn't slow or tender, the way I'd anticipated, but reckless, hungry, almost violent in its urgency. *This is it,* I realized. *She's what I've been missing.* Even while it was happening, I knew I'd never get enough. When it was over, we lay side by side on the pale gray carpet, stunned by our bodies and what they'd done.

"Come back after school," she whispered.

"You'll be at work."

"I'll take the afternoon off. Darren's with the sitter till five-thirty."

That's what I was thinking about around two-twenty in the afternoon, when Tammy Warren knocked on my door.

TAMMY WARREN

MR. M. APOLOGIZED as soon as I sat down.

"Tammy, I want you to know that this isn't my

idea. Mr. Hendricks asked me to conduct an investigation into the disappearance of Paul's posters. As far as I'm concerned, this is pure formality. You're under no suspicion whatsoever."

I was surprised by his kindness. He'd never been nice to me before.

"Thanks," I said. "Ask away."

He stared at the wall clock for ten or fifteen seconds, as if fascinated by the concept of time. He seemed jittery, and I wondered if something was wrong in his personal life. Maybe he was a cocaine addict living in a house with no furniture. Maybe he exposed himself to Cub Scouts.

"All right," he said. "Just for the record. Did you tear down your brother's campaign posters?"

It had been a blue Monday for me. When I got to school that morning, Jason Caputo was waiting by my locker with a bouquet of peach-colored tulips. Seeing him there, looking so lovestruck and pathetic, made me realize how badly I wanted to get out of Winwood. All at once I was sick of everything. I wanted to do something wild—bite the head off a tulip, tell Jason I had a mad crush on his sister. That crazy, desperate feeling had stuck with me the whole day.

"I did it," I told him. "I tore down the posters."

MR. M.

I KNEW SHE WAS lying, but I didn't know why. What could Tammy possibly gain by covering for Tracy?

"Come on," I said. "Stop kidding around."

"I'm not kidding around."

"This is serious, Tammy. You know you'll get suspended."

She nodded gravely.

"This will be the second time in a month. Mr. Hendricks may bar you from the election."

"I deserve it," she said. "My conduct's been reprehensible."

I had no idea what she was trying to pull, and even less interest in figuring it out at that particular moment. It was two-thirty, and I needed to be out of the building by two forty-five. If Tammy wanted to take responsibility for something she hadn't done, that was her prerogative.

"Come on," I said. "Let's go tell it to the Vice-Principal."

TAMMY WARREN

THERE MUST HAVE BEEN eight different Styrofoam cups on Mr. Hendricks's desk, many of them imprinted with crescent-shaped bite marks. I'm not sure how he knew which one to drink from.

"Now this is just my opinion, Tammy, but I think you've got some sort of emotional problem. All this hostility seething inside you."

"It's true," I said. "I'm a very angry person."

He brought his wrist to his nose and sniffed at his watchband. He seemed troubled by the odor and sniffed again.

"Maybe you should get some counseling," he advised. "Find out what's causing you to behave this way."

The hard part was over. He had just suspended me for five days—I could have kissed him—and banned me from the election. Now we were killing time until the bell rang.

"Mr. Hendricks," I said, "do you think it would make sense for me to transfer to a Catholic school?"

MR. M.

I RANG THE BELL and pounded on the door, but Sherry didn't answer. In a matter of seconds, desire turned to dread in my veins.

I waited in front of her house for forty-five minutes that felt like four hours, then gave up and drove to the Blue Lantern, an old man's bar about a mile away.

Between sips of warm beer I fed quarters into the pay phone and listened to her voice on the answering machine. When I tried her office, they told me she'd taken a sick day.

After a while I gave up on the phone and settled into my misery. A rational person might not have blamed Sherry for putting the brakes on, but I was in no mood to be rational. My ribs ached with wanting her; my eyeballs throbbed at the thought of going home to Diane. The last thing I needed just then was a hard slap on the back from Walt Hendricks.

"Jim! We've got to stop meeting like this."

He pulled up a stool beside me and blew a quick kiss to an elderly lady drinking by herself at the other end of the bar. She caught it with one hand and blew him a return kiss with the other. Walt seemed like a different man in the dim, generous light of the Blue Lantern, a dapper gent with an easy charm, no longer the plaid-coated buffoon of the school day.

"I make it a point to be in here by five-thirty no matter what," he explained. "It's the only thing that keeps me sane."

He downed a double bourbon in a single swallow, wincing with pleasure. The funereal bartender refilled his glass, then retreated a few steps in the direction of the cash register.

"So what happened?" I asked.

He sighed. "I gave her five days. Banned her from the election."

"How'd she take it?"

"Fine. Just like last time."

"She's a strange one."

He turned to me with a conspiratorial air.

"I was looking at her, Jim. I think she might have a nice little body underneath those baggy clothes. She's gonna give some pimply kid the surprise of his life."

I shut my eyes and saw Sherry standing in the doorway in that blue shirt, smiling like a bride, her legs lit up by a slanty ray of sunshine. She was moist when I touched her, melting between my fingers.

"Four more years," said Walt. His voice was tired now, drained of enthusiasm. "Four more years and I won't have to suspend anyone ever again."

"You don't like that part of it, do you?"

He traced the rim of his glass with his fingertip, first one way, then in reverse.

"I was a shop teacher for twenty years. The kids loved me. I was Mr. H., just like you. Now they hate my guts. I know what they call me. Styrofoam Walt. Coffee Man." He polished off the rest of his drink and laid a fatherly hand on my shoulder. "Don't believe it when they tell you Administration's the way to go. The classroom, Jim. That's where the magic happens."

He slapped a ten-dollar bill on the bar and told me he had to run.

"Peg's got me on a short leash these days." He blew another kiss to the lady across the bar, then gave a sad laugh. "You know how it is."

Walt's departure had a strangely sobering effect on me. As soon as he was gone, I understood it was time for me to go home too. Diane was waiting, probably starting to worry. I felt tenderly toward her, as if my relationship with her were completely independent of my affair with Sherry.

Twilight had set in by the time I pulled into the driveway. I wasn't really paying attention to the world around me, just trying to screw up my courage for the moment when I walked through the door, back into the life that suddenly seemed bleak and inadequate, a half-decade mistake. If I'd noticed the old Corolla parked in front of our next-door neighbor's house, I might not have been so shocked to see Sherry sitting on my living room couch with a box of Kleenex in her lap, and Diane sitting right next to her with the baby in her arms. All three of them were crying, and my arrival didn't seem to comfort anyone.

9

TAMMY WARREN

I WAS WATCHING my yoga program when Mom got home from work. She shot me a dirty look, then stormed into the kitchen. It was hard for me to imagine my heart as an unfolding flower with her slamming cabinets, banging pots, and heaving those bottomless sighs of exasperation.

She opted for the silent treatment when we sat down to eat. Paul was dining elsewhere, so the meal was quiet as a chess match, two grand masters puzzling over a chicken casserole. After a while I got tired of listening to myself masticate.

"I didn't do it," I told her.

She stabbed angrily at a little green brain of broccoli.

"Mr. Hendricks said you admitted it."

"I lied."

Confusion softened her features.

"Were you covering for someone?"

"Nope."

"Then why would you lie?"

"Because I felt like getting suspended."

I'd underestimated my power to shock my mother. I thought she'd be happy to know I hadn't destroyed images of her son's face.

"But why?" Her question was barely audible, her eyes big and pleading.

A strange pressure gathered in my throat. I shut my eyes and searched for the unfolding flower, but all I came up with was that weird illustration in my Biology textbook, the one that makes the human heart look like a cleanly plucked chicken.

"Because," I told her.

That was the best I could do.

MR. M.

SHERRY NEVER CAME HOME that night. I know this for a fact because I spent something like seven hours in her driveway, waiting like a dog for a glimpse of her.

No words had passed during our brief encounter

in the living room. I stared at Sherry and Diane for a couple of seconds and they stared back, puffy-eyed and hostile. Then I turned around and walked back out to my car.

Desolation gave way to numbness as I drove, and the numbness began to feel oddly like optimism. I headed south on the Parkway for about an hour, stopped at a diner, than turned around and headed back. It's hard to imagine at this remove, but by the time I pulled into Sherry's driveway around ten o'clock, I was fairly certain we'd end up spending the night together. She'd have to come home at some point, I reasoned, and when she did, she'd have to let me in.

How could she not? We were lovers now; the thing that had happened to us was too real, too powerful to deny. It was the kind of miracle you could build a life around, or so it seemed to me then, perched on the ledge of what looked like a new beginning, but turned out to be a long way down.

PAUL WARREN

TAMMY KNOCKED on my door around midnight.

"You up?" she whispered.

"Yeah."

I couldn't see much of her as she moved toward

the foot of my bed, just a white nightgown floating on grainy blackness.

"Did Mom tell you?"

"Tell me what?"

"I got suspended. Five days. I'm out of the election."

"What happened?"

"I told M. and Hendricks I ripped up your posters."

"Did you?"

"No." It offended her that I even had to ask. "It must have been Tracy."

"That's what Lisa thought, too."

"Not that I blame her," Tammy continued. "They were pretty gross."

I didn't argue. By that point I was pretty much sick of them myself. It was Lisa who insisted on going to Hendricks and making a big deal out of it. Of course, she'd done all the work in the first place, so I figured she had the right.

"I don't get it," I said. "Why would you take the fall for Tracy?"

My eyes had partly adjusted to the darkness by then. I could barely make out the pale oval of her face.

"I was serious yesterday. I want to transfer to Immaculate Mary."

It was hard for me to imagine anyone, even devout Catholics, actually wanting to go to a school like that—single sex, with dorky uniforms and nuns for teachers. No football team or marching band or senior prom. For a smart-ass atheist like my sister to volunteer for that world seemed totally perverse.

"Come on," I said.

"Go ahead and laugh."

"I'm not laughing. I just can't imagine why you'd want to do something like that."

Her face snapped into focus just then, wide eyes, a mouth set hard with determination. A whitish hand cast a faint glow against her darkly gleaming hair.

"I'm like Dad," she said. "I want to start all over."

TRACY FLICK

SOMETIMES WHEN I can't sleep and my stomach's all tied up in knots, I think about something I heard on the TV news during last year's presidential election. A panel of experts was discussing the candidates, and one of them said, "The problem with George Bush isn't that he lacks fire-in-the-belly, it's that fire-in-the-belly is all he has."

I'd never heard that expression before and it jarred something loose in me. I remembered how Jack used to tell me I had "fever skin." It seemed to him that I was always running a slight temperature, glowing with extra heat.

"My God," he'd say. "You're burning up."

So now, when I'm wide awake at three in the morning, wondering why I have no close friends, I comfort myself with the thought that I belong to a secret and powerful club—me, George Bush, Madonna, Dan Rather, plus thousands of people you've never heard of—and we're all lying there in separate beds with our eyes wide open and these tiny bonfires blazing in our stomachs, lighting up the night.

MR. M.

IT'S NOT PLEASANT to wake up in your car like that, cold and confused in yesterday's clothes, some terrible truth swimming up from the deep end of your consciousness. I got out and walked to the bottom of the driveway, ostensibly to check for the Corolla, but really just to stretch my legs and get the blood moving through my system. I knew Sherry hadn't come home. The predawn sky had lightened to a dingy gray and my mouth tasted like despair. I was amazed at the speed with which she'd betrayed me.

It's true: despite the fact that I was an adulterer, a man who'd fallen in love—lust, infatuation, whatever; all the words were true—with his wife's best friend, the mother of our godchild, I felt betrayed, and still do.

Emotions won't listen to reason, especially not at five in the morning when there's a damp chill in the air, when your bladder's full and your head seems to have been put on crooked.

There was no alternative but to go home. I needed to shower, put on some fresh clothes, maybe try to explain myself to Diane. But what was I supposed to say? That our marriage had become a weary farce, our efforts to produce a child heightening rather than relieving the staleness of our union? That making love with Sherry had turned me into a different person, someone endowed with a vision of a new and better life, even if that vision seemed already to have gone up in smoke? My wife wasn't a morning person on the best of days, and I didn't figure she'd be too keen on hearing any of this before her first cup of coffee.

The sky was a little brighter and my head a little clearer by the time I turned onto the tree-lined street I'd once expected to be home forever, but which suddenly felt like history, a place where I used to live. I was startled by the sight of Sherry's Corolla still parked the wrong way in front of our neighbor's house, one wheel perched drunkenly on the edge of the curb. (My erroneous guess was that she'd spent the night at her sister's in Green Brook, where she'd frequently sought refuge during the dissolution of her marriage.)

My red gym bag was resting on the front stoop, one

of those sights you know you'll remember for the rest of your life, like fire coming out of an upstairs window of a house down the block, or your mother sobbing in an airport. Inside it were my shaving kit, a towel, a change of clothes, and a note in Diane's handwriting: "Jim—Please don't come inside."

TRACY FLICK

MY MOTHER GOT UP at five in the morning and helped me ice the two hundred cupcakes we'd baked the night before. I planned on handing them out at the main entrance, along with a smile and a gentle reminder of who to vote for. (There were nine hundred plus students at Winwood, but two hundred strained the limits of our kitchen and our patience. I just hoped that none of the people who missed out would hold it against me.)

I was queasy from the chocolate air and not enough sleep, but my mother seemed happy and well rested, like there was nothing in the world she'd rather be doing before sunrise than icing cupcakes to advance my career. She hummed as she frosted, pausing for occasional sips of coffee.

Besides me, my mother didn't have much of a life. She hadn't dated anyone in years and didn't even seem to be looking anymore. She rarely bought new clothes for herself and we didn't travel except to visit colleges and museums. Her only real hobby was writing fan letters to successful women, asking if they had any advice for her "college-bound daughter." We'd received lots of nice responses from people like Pat Schroeder, Anna Quindlen, and Connie Chung, telling me to study hard and dream big dreams, etc. She kept the letters in a file folder, and I sometimes caught her flipping through them with a faraway look in her eyes.

"Mom," I said, "I think I'm going to lose today."

She spread the icing with a smooth swirling motion, finishing with an elegant flourish. She poked a toothpick into the summit of the cupcake, then set it carefully inside the cardboard box.

"No you won't, honey. This time tomorrow you'll be President."

She was always serenely confident of my success, and it never failed to cheer me up.

"You think so?"

She dipped a finger into the icing bowl, then stuck it in her mouth.

"I know so. Tracy Flick's a winner."

When we were done—the cupcakes filled six boxes—I hurried to shower and get dressed. For luck, I wore my boldest red dress, the one that makes people stare.

It's funny to me that I have a reputation as a sexpot,

because I hardly ever feel sexy. My hair is dull and my face is so bland that I stare into the mirror sometimes and feel like bursting into tears. But I have a good body, and in that dress I start to feel like the person everyone seems to think I am, a daring girl with no apologies for anything.

My mother was standing by the refrigerator in jeans and a cardigan, still licking chocolate off her fingers. She'd gotten her boss's permission to start work an hour later than usual.

"Wowee," she said. "You look scrumptious."

I spun in a circle, happy to be admired.

"Come on," she said. "Cupcakes are in the car."

As a precaution, we got to school at seven fifteen, a good half hour before the early birds would start showing up. (I wasn't about to let either of the Warrens beat me to a prime spot by the side entrance.) We'd set up the card table and unpacked two of the boxes when Mr. M.'s car pulled into the teachers' lot over by the temporary classrooms.

I kept my eyes down, pretending to straighten a row of cupcakes, and didn't look up until my mother nudged me with her elbow. Mr. M. was about twenty feet away, a red gym bag in his hand, examining us with an expression of horror and revulsion I doubt I'll ever forget. It was shocking to see him so wild-eyed and disheveled, shirt rumpled and untucked, shoelaces untied. He looked like he'd spent the night in a bus station.

MR. M.

UNTIL I SAW THEM there, standing by that table full of goodies, I swear to God I'd forgotten all about the election. Tracy's red dress brought it all flooding back to me — her lies and threats, Tammy's suspension, the logistical nightmare I was about to face when all I wanted was to curl up under my desk and sleep the day away. I was well aware of the fact that I had not yet showered or combed my hair, and was in no mood to make small talk with Barbara Flick. Tracy smelled blood. I could see it in her smile.

"Mr. M.," she said. "Looks like you could use a cupcake."

10

TRACY FLICK

"ATTENTION!" The word exploded from the intercom speaker, garbled by static and strange gobbling noises. It sounded like someone was trying to eat the microphone. "This is your Vice-Principal speaking!"

A brief riot erupted in my homeroom, as it always did when Mr. Hendricks addressed the school. Wads of paper bounced off the wall near the speaker. Some kids pretended to tear out their hair; others made crosses with their fingers and hissed as though fending off a vampire. Shrieks of mock terror filled the air.

"Oh no!"

"Coffee Man!"

"Hide the Cremora!"

The humor of this ritual eluded me under the best of circumstances, and I happened just then to be suffering from a brutal stomachache, a wriggling knot of pain that made me wonder if the stress of the election had given me an ulcer. I shared a moment of sympathetic eye contact with Mrs. Jardine, who shook her head mournfully at the front of the room, waiting for the outburst to run its course.

"People," she said. "This is for *your* benefit."

Mr. Hendricks cleared his throat with a gross hawking sound, like a cat choking up a hair ball.

"As you know, this is a landmark day for Winwood High, and it . . . ah . . . behooves me to inform you of an important change affecting today's election. Effective this morning, you have only two choices for President. Due to disciplinary proceedings of a confidential nature, Tammy Warren has withdrawn from the race. I'd like to wish the best of luck to our two remaining candidates, Paul Warren and Tracy Flick."

Every face in the room was a question aimed at me. I didn't know what Tammy had done, but I was pretty sure the Warrens had teamed up to pull a fast one at my expense. My stomach hurt so bad it just about killed me to smile.

MR. M.

THE LOGISTICS of a high school election are no laughing matter. At the same time you're educating your students about democracy, you're working to safe-guard the process against fraud. It's sad but true: given half a chance, most kids will cheat to win. They're a lot like adults in this respect.

The voting was scheduled to take place outside the cafeteria during fourth, fifth, and sixth period. We had it down to a science. To obtain a ballot, a student would present an ID and sign a register, at which point his or her name would be crossed out on a master list. The bal-lot would be filled out immediately in our mock voting booth and dropped into a locked, slotted box. The votes would be counted during seventh period, the winner announced during eighth period assembly.

Walt called me into his office immediately after homeroom. He was smiling grimly, dressed in a blue polyester suit apparently meant to simulate denim. In the center of his desk was a fat manila envelope marked "BALLOTS."

"Jim," he said, "I've got a little project for you."

Due to an unusual outbreak of competence in the front office, the ballots had been prepared a week in ad-vance and locked in a secure filing cabinet. Walt had retrieved them that morning only to realize that we'd been betrayed by our own efficiency — Tammy's name appeared on each and every one of them.

"We've got to get rid of her," he said. "It's a night-mare to count these things as it is."

"You want me to type up a new one?"

Walt didn't answer right away. He poked his pinky in his ear and swirled it around with a thoroughness that made me look away.

"I'd hate to waste the paper. We're way the fuck over budget as it is." He examined his pinky for a second or two, then renewed his excavation. "I swear to Christ, people must wipe their butts with letterhead around here."

There were 750 sequentially numbered ballots. While my students caught up with their reading during first and second period, I sat at my desk with a Magic Marker, blacking out Tammy's name with the diligence of an FBI censor. It was tedious, mind-numbing, idiot labor, just what the doctor ordered. I only wished the ledger of my own life could be so easily set aright, with a series of fat black lines drawn neatly through my sins and errors.

TAMMY WARREN

"SUSPENDED" WAS a good word for the way I felt. In between. Nowhere. I had abandoned one part of my life and not yet begun another. I had jumped up and not come down, except in fantasies.

I was possessed by a vision of myself as a Catholic

schoolgirl, Dana's best friend and secret love. In the Immaculate Mary of my mind, we held hands and skipped down the hallway in matching uniforms, causing no consternation among the smiling nuns and shyly beautiful French girls who watched us pass. (For some reason, many of our imaginary schoolmates were French, with heart-shaped faces and silky hair. Their lips were full and pouty and they spoke English with just the slightest trace of an accent.)

Shortly after ten o'clock I got on my bike and rode through the empty streets into the corny, Colonial-style business district of West Plains. The morning was damp and cool, the sky a bright pearly gray. The world seemed to tremble on the edge of spring, and I pedaled as hard as I could, as if I could somehow speed its arrival.

Bells jingled as I walked through the front door of the Little Sally Ann Shop, the store Dana had told me about. Behind the counter, a gray-haired woman with reading glasses pinching the tip of her nose smiled and put down her knitting. She didn't seem surprised to see a girl my age wander in in the middle of a school day.

"Yes, dear?"

I told her that my family had just relocated from California and that I would soon begin classes at Immaculate Mary. Naturally, I was curious about the uniforms.

"Of course," she said. "Come with me."

The skirt was lightweight gray wool, pleated and soft, the blouse stark white with a sweet rounded collar. I'd remembered to wear my own knee socks and saddle shoes, a souvenir from an ill-advised tryout for the jayvee cheerleading squad freshman year.

Smiling at the transformation, I stood before the three-paneled mirror in my new outfit, studying myself from every angle. I looked good. I'll be happy now, I remember thinking. Everything will be better.

"You'll like it at Immaculate," the saleslady told me. "The public schools around here are going down the toilet."

"Oh please," I told her, twisting my hips to flare the skirt. "You don't have to tell *me*."

PAUL WARREN

YOU SEE these pictures all the time, the grinning politician emerging from behind the curtain, flashing a thumbs-up to TV land, and it seems like the most natural thing in the world: in the privacy of the booth, with a clean conscience and boundless optimism, this man has just pulled the lever next to his own name.

I never gave it a second thought until Larry DiBono handed me my ballot that afternoon. I ducked into the goofy "voting booth" they rigged up every year—it was really just a wooden desk surrounded by a wraparound shower curtain—uncapped my pen, and was overcome with disgust. All at once, the idea of voting for myself seemed utterly repugnant. It was selfish and unfair, like a defendant sitting on his own jury, or an author reviewing his own book.

If I can't win this thing without my own vote, I told myself, then I probably don't deserve to be President. I scrawled "None of the Above" across the bottom of the ballot, folded the paper in half, and slipped it into the box.

MR. M.

LARRY DIBONO DROPPED the ballot box on top of my desk. We had thirty-five minutes to tabulate 641 votes, and I was tired. Tired the way you might expect a person to be who had spent the night in his car. Tired the way you get when you know you haven't even begun to face up to the gravity of a bad situation. I scowled at the box.

"Maybe we should just get some lighter fluid and torch the thing," I said. "Save us a lot of trouble."

Larry laughed uneasily, more startled than amused. Being an election monitor was not something he took lightly.

"You want me to look for Mr. Hendricks?" he asked.

We'd already wasted ten valuable minutes waiting for Walt outside the cafeteria. The regulations stipulated that three people had to be present at all times during the handling of the ballots—the SGA President, the faculty advisor, and the Vice-Principal.

"I'll go find him," I said. "In the meantime, why don't you get started on your count."

Larry hesitated, unable to conceal his discomfort. He was a straight arrow who believed in following rules, but he was also a brownnoser who derived great pleasure from obeying orders. As usual, the brownnoser won out.

"Are you sure it's okay?"

"Sure," I said, handing him the key to the box. "Just don't light any matches."

I can still remember how good it felt to step into the hallway, as if my body had somehow sensed the danger packed inside that box of votes. The feeling of freedom—of reprieve—was so intense that I had to stop myself from breaking into a run, sprinting like a fugitive down that gleaming tunnel of lockers and linoleum and Tracy for President, bursting through glass doors into the safety of the hazy afternoon.

Instead of running away, I permitted myself to indulge in the cheap luxury of hope. Maybe Sherry's come to her senses, I thought. Maybe she misses me and wants to get together. After all, you can't expect a situation as complicated as ours to fall into place without a hitch, etc. It's painful to look back on a moment like that, to watch yourself play the dual role of con man and dupe, gulping down the snake oil you've just brewed for your own consumption.

Ducking into the phone booth around the corner from Walt's office, I reached into my pocket and fished out a handful of change, including several quarters. This struck me as a good omen, because I almost never have quarters on hand when I need them. My fingers trembled as I pushed the buttons.

Sherry wasn't home and she hadn't gone to work. The only other place I could think to try was my own house.

"Hello?" She answered like a guest, tentative and too polite, but her voice made everything real again.

"I love you," I told her.

The silence on the other end was frosty and careful, not what I needed it to be.

"Don't," she said. "You know it's not true."

"It's the only true thing I know anymore."

I waited again, breathing in the teenage fragrances of gum and sweet perfume wafting up from the mouthpiece.

"I can't do it, Jim."

"Do what?"

"We made a mistake. Let's not make it worse."

"A *mistake*?" The word was so wrong it was almost comical. "That was no mistake."

This time the pause was longer, more substantial. "I was lonely," she said. "You took advantage."

A new kind of bitterness flooded into my mouth. It was like nothing I'd ever tasted in my life.

"*Me?* I took advantage of you? Do you remember what you were wearing?"

I heard a sharp intake of breath, followed by a dial tone and the merciless voice of the phone company. *If you'd like to make a call, please hang up and try again . . . If you'd like to make a call . . .*

I stood in a kind of trance in the upright coffin of the booth listening to that inane recording over and over. I might have passed the rest of the afternoon in there if Walt hadn't shoved open the Plexiglas door and grabbed me by the shoulder.

"Jesus, Jim. Here you are. I've been looking all over."

When we got back to my room, Larry had the votes sorted into three neat piles of approximately equal height. He seemed relieved to see us.

"Well?" said Walt. "What's the verdict?"

Larry looked shocked, as if Walt had just inquired as to the size of his penis.

"I—I'm not supposed to tell you. We're each supposed to make an independent count."

Walt shook his head slowly, with a combination of disgust and admiration.

"DiBono," he said, "you're a real piece of work."

Larry's ears turned an unfortunate shade of red, but he showed more backbone than I expected.

"Those are the rules as they were explained to me, Mr. Hendricks. If they've changed in any way . . ."

"DiBono, we're not choosing the fucking Pope here. The fate of the world doesn't exactly hang in the balance. So I'd appreciate it if you spared me the bullcrap, okay?"

Larry hung his head.

"It was a squeaker," he said. "I've got Tracy by a vote."

TRACY FLICK

THE SUSPENSE WAS killing me. How was I supposed to concentrate on Trig when my political future was hanging in the balance?

I clutched my stomach and moaned. A lot of kids stared at me, but Mr. Sperigno just kept scribbling on the blackboard. My second moan was unignorable. Mr. S. turned around, eyeing me with a certain amount of skepticism.

"Someone call a priest," he said. "I think there's a demon in our midst."

He didn't really believe that I was suffering from "acute gastritis," but he wrote me a pass to the nurse's office anyway. Mr. S. is good that way. Some of the other teachers will quiz you about your symptoms right in front of the class, as if they're trained medical professionals.

By coincidence, Mr. M.'s room happened to be right on my way to the nurse's office. How could I not stop by the door and take a peek?

It's always disappointing to see stuff like that in real life. You imagine a big scoreboard, your name in lights, crowds of reporters milling around. But what you get is Mr. M. sitting at his desk, playing solitaire with the ballots, while Larry and Mr. Hendricks stand a few feet apart by the window, sharing a lovely view of the parking lot. So much for democracy in action.

I had to wait a long time before Larry finally turned around. I waved and his face lit up in a dopey smile. Larry had a crush on me—a big, hopeless crush. He asked me out on a regular basis—I always said no—and wrote me the kind of letters you'd die to get from Mr. Right, but are totally embarrassing coming from anybody else, especially a sweet dorky guy like Larry. Despite the fact that I'd broken his heart a hundred times over, we'd somehow managed to remain on pretty good terms. He was one of the few people at Winwood I knew I could count on.

I crossed my fingers by my ears and mouthed the word, "Well?"

Larry glanced from side to side. M. was counting the votes. Hendricks was still memorizing the view. Larry flashed me a double thumbs-up.

"Really?" I mouthed.

He nodded, eyes wide with confirmation.

You know that moment when they announce the winner of a beauty pageant? When Miss Texas or whoever suddenly realizes she's Miss America and all she can do is scream and weep and hug the losers? I had mine in the hallway, with no one to hug but myself.

MR. M.

LARRY HAD SORTED the votes into three categories—Paul, Tracy, and Disregard.

If you want to get technical, Disregard actually won the election with 230 votes. About half of these were write-in votes for Tammy—which tells you something about her support—and most of the remainder were split among celebrity write-ins—Bart Simpson, Shannen Doherty, Long Dong Silver—and true confessions—I'm Gay, I Had an Abortion, I Want to Die.

Judging from the ballots, a plurality of our students were scared, angry, lonely, and in desperate need of role models.

My count of the other two piles worked out exactly the same as Larry's: Tracy had won the election by a single vote, 206 to 205. I had her last two votes in my hand and was about to announce my tally when I happened to look up and see her face in the window of my classroom door.

The sight of her at that moment irritated me in a way I can't fully explain. Part of it was that she was spying, but mainly it was her expression that made me furious. She was wide-eyed and jubilant, like she somehow already knew she'd won the election. And innocent, too. Looking at her, you'd have no idea she'd scratched and clawed her way to the top, lying and cheating when necessary. You'd think she was just a sweet teenage girl who deserved every good thing that had ever happened to her.

She realized I was staring and darted out of sight. Larry and Walt were standing at the window, facing away from me. As quietly as I could, I closed my fist around the two ballots in my hand, crumpling them into a compact wad that I deposited in the wastebasket beneath my desk.

"Larry," I said, "I think we have a problem."

11

MR. M.

I REGRETTED IT IMMEDIATELY, but even that was too late. Larry and Walt were watching; there seemed no recourse but to finish what I'd started.

"I've got Paul by one. Two-oh-five to two-oh-four."

"That can't be." Larry was adamant. "I double-checked. Tracy won by a vote."

"Maybe I'm wrong," I told him, "but that's my tally."

Walt frowned at the clock. Fifteen minutes remained in the period. I expected him to throw a tantrum, but he just withdrew a handkerchief from his coat pocket and blew his nose.

"Tell me," he said, pausing to switch nostrils. "Why does everything have to be such a goddam melodrama around here?"

Walt usurped my desk to count the votes, so I had little choice but to join Larry by the window. He didn't look at me or say a word, but I could sense his hostility, the angry bewilderment of a teenager who suddenly suspects that the fix is in from the adult world. Under different circumstances, I might have tried to comfort him.

At least for the moment, though, Larry's agitation had the paradoxical effect of calming my nerves. Seeing myself through his eyes brought me back to the rock-bottom reality of the situation: he was the student; I was the teacher. If it came down to my word against his—absent any physical evidence—I would win.

For several minutes, the only sounds in the room were Walt's heavy breathing and the whispery shuffle of paper. At the far end of the parking lot, students in gym clothes volleyed lazily on the tennis courts, reaching and swatting at a swooping green dot. It was ballet from this distance, pointless and beautiful.

My regrets just then ran in a couple of directions. I wished I hadn't done what I'd done, and I also wished I'd thought of a less obvious place to dispose of the ballots. Even my pants pocket would have been safer than the trash can. But the truth, of course, was that I hadn't thought at all. I just saw my opportunity and took it.

Walt cleared his throat and stood up.

"Jim's right. Paul Warren's our new President by a

single vote. I can't remember an election this close in all my years at Winwood."

Larry turned slowly away from the window, shaking his head with a bitter certainty that froze the moment.

"No way. It doesn't make sense."

"Sorry." Walt dismissed him with a shrug. "My figures work out exactly the same as Jim's. Two-oh-five for Paul, two-oh-four for Tracy."

Larry wasn't buying it.

"How many Disregards?"

Walt referred to the palm of his left hand.

"Two hundred thirty."

"See?" Larry spread his arms wide for emphasis. He was turning into a lawyer right in front of our eyes. "It doesn't add up. You counted six hundred thirty-nine votes. But our ledger shows that six hundred and forty-one people voted."

Walt looked pained, as though he were attempting the math in his head.

"Two votes are missing," Larry added helpfully. "You can check the register."

"He's right," I said. "Two people must have pocketed their ballots in the booth. There's really no way for us to prevent that."

"They were *there*," Larry insisted. "I counted six hundred and forty-one votes."

I patted him on the shoulder, a fatherly and forgiving gesture.

"It happens, Larry. People make mistakes."

He glared at me, offended by my touch.

"*I* didn't make a mistake. Every vote was there when you sat down."

"Whoa." Walt's voice carried a sharp note of warning. "Easy, DiBono. Don't say anything you'll regret in the morning."

Even then, Larry wouldn't back down. He was starting to scare me.

"I'm telling you, Mr. Hendricks. Every vote was accounted for."

"Okay," said Walt. "Take it easy. Let's use our heads here. Where could they have gone?"

Larry drilled me with a look of undisguised contempt.

"Under the blotter," he said. "Maybe they slid there by accident."

Walt lifted the blotter and shook his head.

"Check inside the ballot box," I suggested.

The bell rang, signaling the end of seventh period. Walt turned the box upside down and gave it a shake. Nothing fell out.

"Under the desk." Larry spoke quickly, knowing we were pressed for time.

A powerful adrenaline rush shot through my body

as Walt knelt to the floor. For the first time all day, my head was clear. For the first time in what felt like months, I made a smart decision.

"Don't forget the garbage can," I called out.

Walt stood up after only a few seconds had passed, not long enough for him to make a thorough search of the wastebasket, which was filled with a day's worth of wrappers, memos, and paper cups. He dusted off his pants and straightened his tie.

"Sorry, gents. Negative on both counts."

PAUL WARREN

IT WAS LIKE the Oscars, only worse. Tracy and I were made to sit together on stage in front of the whole school so everyone could watch our reactions when Larry announced the winner. It was a needlessly cruel arrangement, and I vowed to abolish it if I were lucky enough to be elected.

Tracy seemed like a different person now that the voting was over, no longer the fierce opponent I'd come to fear and dislike in recent weeks. She smiled as I took my seat and graciously offered her hand.

"However this turns out," she told me, "I want you to know that you've run a wonderful campaign. It's been an honor competing with you."

I shook her hand without hesitation, moved by the generosity of the gesture. It's probably a defect in my personality, this eagerness to forgive and forget.

"It's been a long road," I said. "I'm kind of glad it's finally over."

"Not me." She took a moment to survey the rows upon rows of faces spread out below us. "I'll miss all the excitement."

"I guess I like it dull."

"Huh." She made a face. "Your life doesn't seem all that dull to me."

"All this glitz and glamour's just a smokescreen," I told her with a laugh. "At heart, I'm a very boring person."

She leaned closer. Her expression was hard to read.

"I get so jealous watching you and Lisa in the hall-way. It's been a long time since anyone kissed me like that."

I tried not to show it, but I was startled by her remark. Not only because she'd been watching me and Lisa, but also because I was pretty sure she was referring to Mr. Dexter. He'd disappeared overnight, without a word of explanation, but everyone knew that it had something to do with Tracy. In one story, her mother caught them fucking in her bedroom; in another, a janitor opened the door on a supply-room blow job. Neither story sounded quite right to me, but even so, it was a strange moment to raise such a delicate subject, the two of us on display in front of close to a thousand people.

I felt guilty, too, because I didn't really deserve the benefit of even that much of her trust. Like everyone else at Winwood, I'd gotten a lot of mileage out of last year's scandal, mostly at Tracy's expense. Mr. Dexter was one of the most popular teachers at school; for weeks my friends and I had obsessed over the riddle of his behavior.

"How could he fall for Tracy?" we asked ourselves over and over, in the incredulous tone we reserved for unsolved mysteries of the highest order. "*For Tracy!*"

But just then, to my immense surprise, I thought I understood what he saw in her, aside from that amazing body. It was something that had never occurred to me before: she was unhappy. On stage that afternoon, this simple fact struck me with the unmistakable force of truth. Tracy Flick needed someone to cheer her up. So did Lisa, now that I thought about it; so did Tammy and my mother and my father. Maybe that's what we look for in the people we love, the spark of unhappiness we think we know how to extinguish . . .

My reverie dissolved in a sudden burst of applause as Mr. M. came trudging up the steps to join us on stage, looking pale and haggard. I tried to make eye contact with him, but he shuffled past us without a glance and took his place behind the podium. Tracy grabbed my hand.

"I'm so nervous," she whispered. "I think I'm going to wet my pants."

TAMMY WARREN

I LEANED MY BIKE against a tree and sat down on the curb across the street from the main entrance, momentarily startled by the sight of my skinny legs poking out from the skirt. I straightened my droopy socks and wiped some dirt from the tip of my shoe.

It felt good to be far away from Winwood, the treadmill of familiar faces and boring routines, the straitjacket of people's expectations. The school always reminded me of a warehouse or factory, this long low rectangle set far apart from everything, surrounded by an enormous parking lot and acres of athletic fields. The building itself is plain and impersonal, with no real ornamentation except these gleaming ventilation units rising like silver mushrooms from the flat roof.

Immaculate Mary was built on a more human scale, a two-story brick building on a tree-lined street near the edge of downtown Cranwood, with a sloping lawn and a flight of wide concrete steps leading up to the main entrance. Above the door was a marble frieze of the Virgin

Mary gazing sadly upon the world, the wrinkles of her robe so real-seeming you could hardly believe they were made of stone.

Aside from Jason, who didn't really count, I doubted anyone would miss me in all of Winwood, least of all Lisa. I would disappear and that would be it. No one would stop by my locker and scratch their head, wondering where I'd gone. I was tired of that, tired of being Nobody, Paul's Sister, the Girl Who Made the Speech. All I wanted was a chance to go somewhere new, make some real friends, be my true self. It didn't seem like too much to ask of the world.

The bell rang at two-thirty, and the girls of Immaculate Mary came streaming out the door and down the steps, fanning across the lawn like a flock of blue-gray-and-white birds, heading for the fleet of school buses parked at the corner. The afternoon swelled with their voices and laughter.

I picked myself up and strolled across the street into the thick of the crowd. Moving against the flow, I threaded my way through a maze of unfamiliar faces—black, white, and brown girls, girls with pimples, smiling girls, fat girls, all of them dressed like me, all of us part of the same happy exit.

Dana was standing at the base of the stairs, talking to a chubby girl with frizzy red hair. I stopped for a few seconds to admire her and gather my courage. She wore black tights instead of knee socks, and had a navy cardigan draped over her shoulders, the empty sleeves flopping across her chest. One of her shirt cuffs was un-buttoned, and it flapped around her wrist every time she moved her hand.

I walked right up and tapped her on the shoulder. Her mouth opened slowly into a question she couldn't seem to ask. The red-haired girl looked worried.

"Oh my God," said Dana.

"I know," I told her.

TRACY FLICK

I SHOULD'VE REALIZED I was in trouble as soon as Mr. M. made his entrance. It was Larry's job to an-nounce the winner, and he wouldn't have surrendered the opportunity to speak my name and hug me in front of the whole school unless something was seriously amiss.

But who was thinking of Larry or trouble? I was too busy concentrating on my acceptance speech, mak-ing sure I struck the right notes of gratitude and mod-esty and mentioned the names of all the people whose help and support I might need in the future. Though I'm told I'm a natural, public speaking has never come easily to me. The prospect of doing it always puts me in a weird hyper state. I can't really focus on anything but the words in my head; the rest of the world dissolves into a thick dreamy fog.

"Some contests are so well fought it seems unfair for someone to have to win and someone to have to lose." Mr. M.'s voice reached my ears with a wobbly quaver, as though he were speaking through water instead of air. "Both candidates before you are highly qualified; both embody the virtues of leadership and integrity we expect and deserve in a school President. Either one of them, I believe, would make an excellent chief executive."

God, I thought, *would you get on with it! Shake Paul's hand,* I reminded myself. *Walk slowly to the podium. Try not to look too happy . . .*

"That said," he continued, "the whole point of an election is to choose a winner, and that you have done, by the margin of a single vote. You the people have spoken; you the people have selected your next President."

He withdrew the envelope from his back pocket and began tearing it open. I'm not sure why they do it like that, maybe to make the whole process seem more official or something. *Smile at your constituents. Thank them for this incredible honor . . .*

"Without further ado, it's my pleasure to announce the next President of Winwood High. And the winner is—"

He hesitated just a second or two at the crucial juncture, long enough for me to completely lose my patience. In that unexpected bubble of silence, as if my name had already been called, I rose from my chair and stood smiling in my red dress in front of the entire school.

"—Paul Warren!"

12

MR. M.

I SMILED like a bad actor through Paul's acceptance speech and clapped along with everyone else. You go on autopilot at moments like that, blanking out all the things you can't possibly afford to think about, knowing you'll have time enough later for shame and regret.

When it was over, all I wanted was to flee the mess I'd made, to rush out of the building like waking from a bad dream, but I was too careful for that. I forced myself to return to my classroom and retrieve the missing ballots. There was no getting around it. As long as they existed, I was vulnerable.

It seemed like a simple enough operation—reach in, grab, and go. Once in my possession, the ballots could be disposed of in any number of ways: I could burn them, drop them down a storm drain, rip them into confetti, flush them down a toilet.

Detective stories are right about one thing, though: once you've committed a crime, nothing is simple. The whole world bends to your exposure. Before you know it, you're on the eleven o'clock news, wearing a jacket on your head.

The moment I reached into the can, someone knocked on the door. I withdrew my hand as carefully as possible, praying as I turned that it wasn't Walt or Larry. Luck was with me. Paul and Lisa smiled through the window, their faces glowing with triumph. I signaled for them to come in.

Lisa hung back a step as Paul marched up to my desk and thrust out his hand. It was cool and dry, a striking contrast to my own.

"Thanks, Mr. M. If it wasn't for you, none of this would have happened."

"Don't thank me," I muttered. "You earned this on your own."

"It was her," he said, reaching for Lisa's hand. "She was the heart and soul of this campaign."

Lisa seemed giddy, like she'd been drinking champagne.

"I can't believe we pulled it off. By a single vote, it's so crazy. I almost feel sorry for Tracy."

With the tip of my shoe, I nudged the wastebasket farther under my desk. The ballots were huge in my mind, as obvious as money.

"It can't be easy for her," I said. "She's a real competitor."

Paul's face clouded over with sympathy. "I tried to talk to her, but she wouldn't even look at me."

Lisa gave a small shudder, hissing sharply through her front teeth.

"It was *so* embarrassing, the way she stood up like that."

"Like what?"

She seemed surprised by my question.

"When you announced Paul's name, Tracy stood up. Didn't you hear everyone laughing?"

"I missed it," I said. "So much was happening at once."

An awkward silence overtook the conversation. I had a feeling they expected something from me.

"Well . . . congratulations." I rose to my feet. "To both of you. I look forward to working with you next year."

I stuck out my hand, but Paul didn't take it. A bashful smile seeped across his face.

"Mr. M.," he said, "could I give you a hug?"

How could I say no? I stepped forward and limply

accepted his embrace. I felt small in his arms, hollow when he slapped me on the back.

"Thanks so much," he whispered.

I saw them to the door, checked both ways to make sure the coast was clear, then hurried back to my desk to finish what I'd started.

The only explanation for what happened next is that my nerves were shot. I couldn't think at all, let alone straight. Instead of reaching for the ballots, I slumped forward onto the desk, resting my forehead on the cool green of the blotter. It felt good to close my eyes and forget.

I woke with a start a few minutes later. Walt was clutching my shoulder, grinning like a madman.

"Jimbo! Caught you napping!"

"Not really," I mumbled. I had to stop myself from swatting at his arm. "Just gathering my thoughts."

"Come on," he said. "It's been a long day. Let me buy you a drink."

"No thanks. I've got some quizzes to grade."

His face softened into a pout even as his fingers tightened on my arm.

"Come on, Jimbo. Don't make me beg."

JOE DELVECCHIO

I'M THE HEAD of Maintenance. I supervise the crew, purchase the supplies, sign off on the time sheets. It's not my job to clean the toilets or empty the wastebaskets.

What happened that afternoon, Howie Garber took a two-hour liquid lunch and came back shitfaced, ranting about his mother. I yelled a little, then sent him back to my office to sleep it off.

Howie's like a lot of guys on my crew, a good worker when he's not pissed off at the world. You might be pissed off, too, if you were a forty-year-old janitor who lived with your mother and spent your days cleaning the school you used to attend and the kids snicker behind your back 'cause you're overweight and your pants have a tendency to slide down and expose the crack of your ass. I tell him all the time, "Howie, pull up your goddam pants. Have a little dignity." So he gets drunk a few times a year and sleeps it off in my office.

That's a major part of my job, putting out these employee brushfires. Eddie won't work with Dinger 'cause he farts too much. Ellis refuses to tuck in his shirt. Lou Fillipo gets into a shoving match with a football player who steps on his mop. Steve Piasecki gets caught stealing a carton of erasers, don't ask me why. Stupid, petty shit like that, pointless rebellions.

So anyway, that's why I'm on trash patrol that afternoon. Because it's Howie's job and Howie's fast asleep in my office, recuperating from lunch and his mother who won't get off his back. And the truth is, I don't mind cleaning toilets and emptying wastebaskets every now and then. It's a welcome break from the paperwork that seems to take up more and more of my time. Not to mention that you shouldn't ask someone else to do shitwork if you're not willing to do it yourself.

I can tell you one thing: Howie was a lot more on my mind than Tracy when I walked into McAllister's classroom. I knew she'd lost the election, but I figured it might do her some good in the long run. If you asked me, winning meant too much to her, like she herself was worthless without all her awards and prizes.

This attitude came straight from her mother. They're my tenants and they're both good people, but my own personal feeling was that Barbara pushed her daughter too goddam hard. The girl didn't have any friends, and she didn't have any fun. I thought it might loosen her up a little to find out that losing wasn't the end of the world.

What happened is this: I grabbed the basket, flipped it over, and shook the contents into a heavy-duty plastic bag I was dragging from room to room. A couple of balled-up papers missed the opening and landed on the floor. I'm not really sure what possessed me to pick them up and see what they were. Some combination of boredom and curiosity, I guess. I like to know what people are up to.

One of the papers was a memo about a teacher's meeting. The other was actually two papers, both of them election ballots with an X next to Tracy's name. It didn't seem like a big deal at first. The election was over, so maybe the ballots get tossed. But that didn't seem right once I thought about it. It would take more than one little trash can to hold all the ballots from a schoolwide election. Just to be on the safe side, I smoothed them out and tucked them into my shirt pocket.

MR. M.

THE BLUE LANTERN was dark and restful, the same as the day before. Walt and the elderly lady traded kisses through the air; the expressionless bartender poured without speaking, as though administering a sacrament. Walt and I touched glasses.

"Careful," he told me. "You'll be a regular before you know it."

There was a hopeful note in his warning, and the image it conjured made me laugh in appreciation.

"We'll be like Cliff and Norm."

He didn't get the allusion, so I tried to explain.

"You know, the guys on *Cheers*. The fat one and the postal worker."

This time he managed a wan smile as he swirled the bourbon in his glass, holding it at eye level for a better look.

"I wonder what got into DiBono," he said. "He's not usually such a prick."

"Beats me. Maybe he was embarrassed to make a mistake."

Walt's shrug could have meant anything.

"Personally," he said, "I'd have preferred Flick."

"Really?"

He put down his glass and transferred his hand to my wrist. His eyes were bright, his voice confidential.

"Jesus, Jim, you ever see the ass on that girl?" He shook his head in silent tribute. "It would almost be worth losing your job for a caboose like that."

After everything that had happened, I didn't have the heart for this sort of conversation. Walt must have seen me cringe. He let go of my wrist and swiped wearily at the air.

"I'm sixty-one years old," he told me. "I have to take my thrills where I find them."

JOE DELVECCHIO

I GAVE HOWIE a lift home at five o'clock. He was groggy, still only half sober, and didn't say a word until we pulled up in front of his house.

"Sorry," he mumbled. "Won't happen again."

"I hope not. You're not much use to me drunk."

"I mean it, Joe." The car filled up with the sour reek of his breath. "I'll make it up to you."

"I know, Howie. See you tomorrow."

I watched him climb the front steps, hitch up his pants, and disappear into his house. What did he tell his mother on these nights when he came home carless, stinking of schnapps and peanuts? Did he hang his head and apologize? Or did he storm into his room, slamming the door behind him? All I knew was that he would be back at work the next day, clean-shaven and repentant, and the kids would snicker behind his back, and the whole cycle would begin all over again.

That's what I thought about on my way home. The ballots didn't even cross my mind until I pulled into the driveway and saw Tracy sitting on the front porch steps with Larry DiBono. I was glad to see her hanging out with kids her own age.

I parked the car, locked the garage door, and wandered back around front. The two of them looked so gloomy you might have thought they were boyfriend and girlfriend on the verge of a nasty breakup. They moved apart to clear a path for me, but I paused at the base of the steps.

"What's up, princess?"

Tracy had changed out of her dress, into jeans and a T-shirt. She sniffled and tried to give me a smile.

"I lost." There was a small catch in her voice, like she might start crying again. "I lost by one stupid vote."

Larry studied me for a second or two, trying to size me up.

"Two votes were missing," he said bitterly. "I counted them and then they disappeared."

"Two votes for Tracy?"

I knew the answer before he nodded. I used to be a cop, and the cop part of me was already hearing sirens. I reached into my pocket and showed them what I found.

MR. M.

I WENT HOME that night. There was nowhere else to go.

Diane met me at the door like the perfect wife in a fifties sitcom, wearing an apron over her prettiest dress. The house smelled of perfume and roasted chicken.

"I'm glad you came back," she told me.

Her smile was tense, but undeniably real. It still hurt me to think of Sherry, but the ache had receded to a distant throb. My need for her was like a fever that had broken.

"Diane—" I began.

"Not tonight." She touched a finger lightly to my lips. "Tonight we're calling a truce. We're not going to talk about it."

We ate by candlelight in the dining room, using cloth napkins and our good china. Diane poured the wine and kept the conversation doggedly afloat, asking where I wanted to go on vacation, what I thought about Paul Tsongas, and would I please explain again what was so funny about *Seinfeld*. Her performance was somehow transparent and convincing at the same time, like she wanted me to see how easy it was to cram the pieces of our lives back into their battered old boxes.

"So," she said, "how was your day at school?"

"We had the election."

"The election?" She laughed out loud, as though the election were a private joke we'd been sharing for months. "How could I have forgotten?"

"I forgot, too."

This was the closest either of us had come to acknowledging the previous day's events, but she chose to ignore the opening.

"Well? Aren't you going to tell me who won?"

I stared down at the bones on my plate and considered telling her what I'd done. But even then, barely five hours later, the act no longer seemed real to me. In my heart of hearts, I did not believe that I was the kind of man who would stoop so low as to fix a high school election, and I didn't want anyone else to think I was that kind of man, either.

"Jim?" she said.

"Tracy," I told her.

13

MR. M.

I DROVE TO SCHOOL the next morning and parked in my usual space. I had considered taking the day off, but decided instead to reimmerse myself in the daily routine. The new morning seemed to hold out a promise, if not of absolution, then at least of a second chance.

Walt's secretary buttonholed me just inside the main entrance. Hilda was a nasty, bitter woman on the best of days, so I didn't know what to make of her friendly smile, the light touch of her hand on my arm.

"You're wanted in the office," she told me.

"Okay. I'll be there in a minute."

"No," she said. "He wants to see you now."

So that was how it ended for me—quickly, before I even had a chance to start over. Tracy and Barbara Flick, Joe Delvecchio, and Larry DiBono were all crowded into Walt's office, waiting for my arrival. Tracy burst into tears the moment I walked in. Barbara Flick wrapped both arms around her daughter, but kept her tired, haunted eyes on me.

"Shame," she whispered, and I thought for a second she was saying my name. "Shame."

Larry DiBono measured me with a teenager's pure-hearted hatred, while beside him, Joe Delvecchio conducted a thorough examination of his cuticles. Walt sat behind his desk with a coffee cup in one hand and a pair of wrinkled ballots in the other. Any hope I had of receiving the benefit of the doubt from my new drinking buddy vanished with his first words.

"Mr. McAllister," he said, "I think you've got some explaining to do."

Before I could begin, Larry stood up and headed for the door. I stepped aside to make room for his exit, but he turned on his way out and spit in my face from a distance of about six inches. His saliva struck me in the forehead and dribbled down my eyelid and the side of my nose. It felt like hot oil splattered across my skin, but I couldn't seem to bring myself to reach up and wipe it off.

PAUL WARREN

I GOT TO BE President for a Night. I guess that's like
Queen for a Day or something.

When Mr. Hendricks called me out of homeroom, I
figured he wanted to extend his congratulations and fill
me in on my new responsibilities. It didn't even occur to
me that something might be wrong until I opened his
office door and walked into a dense cloud of gloom.

M. and Hendricks were there; so were Tracy and her
mother. One of them looked more upset than the next,
and I couldn't help thinking that something awful must
have happened, that there'd been an accident somewhere involving a member of my family. Mr. Hendricks
pointed to an empty chair.

"Take a seat, son. The excrement just had a head-on
collision with the cooling unit."

I nodded to Mr. M. as I sat down, but he didn't ac-
knowledge my presence. The Flicks also ignored me,
staring intently at Mr. Hendricks, who was muttering
under his breath as he wrestled with a container of
Tylenol. He finally managed to line up the arrows,
and the cap flew off with a champagne pop, spinning
end over end like a flipped coin until it bounced off
the wall above Mr. M.'s head and landed on the floor
with a soft *click*. Nobody moved to pick it up. Mr.
Hendricks shook a couple of pills into his hand and

swallowed them with a nasty grimace and a mouthful of coffee.

"Jesus," he said. "It didn't used to be such a project to take a couple of aspirin."

Hendricks turned to M.; M. sighed heavily and turned to me. I glanced at the Flicks, thinking how embarrassing it must be for Tracy, having to sit there holding hands with her mother in front of three people she hardly knew.

"Paul," said Mr. M., "you didn't really win the election."

He paused for my reaction, but I didn't protest or ask him to repeat himself. For some reason, this revelation didn't shock me nearly as much as it should have. Winning the election had seemed unreal to me. Having it taken away felt almost normal.

"I'm sorry," he said, and his voice cracked with emotion. "I can't tell you how sorry."

He kept talking, trying to explain what he'd done, but I had a hard time following the details. All I could think about was Lisa, and how badly she was going to take the news.

TRACY FLICK

MR. HENDRICKS CALLED a special first-period assembly to clear up the whole stupid mess. It was basically just a repeat of the day before, except that this time Larry was going to announce the winner, which was the way it was supposed to have been in the first place.

Paul was really good about it. If I'd been in his position, you can bet I wouldn't have agreed to sit on stage in front of the entire student body and have a major honor ripped right out of my hands.

I didn't feel as happy or as vindicated as I expected to. I was relieved, of course, and eager to take possession of what was rightfully mine, but a lot of the joy had been sucked out of my victory. It's just so creepy to discover that you have a blood enemy, someone who's willing to do just about anything to destroy you.

There was something else, too, something I wished I hadn't been forced to admit to myself. On some deep, mysterious level, despite the actual outcome of the election, I still felt like a loser. Nothing was ever going to erase the memory of yesterday's defeat, the moment when I stood up by mistake and was laughed at by hundreds of people. There was something true in that laughter, a truth I felt would taint every good thing in my life for years to come.

Paul laughed softly to himself as the last few stragglers wandered into the auditorium and found their seats.

"You want to know something funny?" he asked.

"What?"

"I didn't vote for myself."

"What?" I was stunned. "You voted for me?"

He shook his head.

"For 'None of the Above.' I can't really explain it. I guess I just lost my nerve."

The last puff of air leaked out of my deflated balloon.

"So it was a tie," I said.

"It was what it was. You won by a vote, fair and square."

Just then Larry came bounding up the steps like a comedian, flashing me a jubilant grin as he took his place behind the podium. In an excited voice, he began to explain about the recount and yesterday's erroneous result. He somehow managed to go into great detail without once mentioning Mr. M. and the unbelievably sleazy thing he'd done. I must have spaced out while he blathered on, because I just sat there for a few seconds after he announced the winner, not even realizing that he'd already called my name.

MR. M.

WHEN YOU HAVE tenure it's not that easy to lose your job. There's a union, and they go to bat for people in all sorts of hot water. Given that the only evidence against me was circumstantial, there's a pretty decent chance I could have denied everything and gotten away with it.

In retrospect, maybe that's what I should have done. Maybe I shouldn't have let one impulsive decision destroy my vocation, the work to which I'd devoted my entire adult life. Maybe I should have stood firm and denied whatever charges the Administration tried to bring against me.

That morning, though, from the moment I entered Walt's office, nothing was clearer to me than the fact that I'd forfeited my right to call myself a teacher. I had been caught violating the closest thing I knew to a sacred trust. My days at Winwood were over.

I didn't bother to clean my desk or take one last tour of the halls. I just walked out to my car in a slow daze of grief and drove home at a crawl of about fifteen miles an hour, as though I'd suddenly become elderly, distrustful of my reflexes.

The rest of the morning was given over to my letter of resignation. It wasn't long, but I must have written it a dozen different ways. The final version went like this:

Effective immediately, I am resigning my position as teacher of History and Social Studies at Winwood High School. I take this action with a deep sadness in my heart.

The nine years I've spent at Winwood have been among the happiest and most productive of my life. I only hope the modest good I've done in these years will not be permanently obscured by the shame I've brought upon myself with my recent actions.

Regretfully,
James T. McAllister

"P.S.," I concluded. "My replacement will find lesson plans for the remainder of the year in my top right-hand drawer."

I sealed the letter in a plain white envelope and started out for the mailbox. It was close to noon, and my timing was unfortunate. The elementary school at the corner had just recessed for lunch, and I had to wade through a sea of hungry kids surging toward home. Exhilarated by their hour of freedom, they ran and shoved their way past me as though I were invisible, laughing and yelling with delight.

Like them, I carried the rhythm of the school day in my blood. I dropped the letter down the slot and knew for certain I was lost.

TAMMY WARREN

By the time I got back to school, Mr. M. was gone and the furor over the election was already starting to feel like old news. I must say, though, that my return caused something of a stir.

There wasn't an actual dress code at Winwood. For the most part, people wore jeans, the baggier the better. Boys favored rugby shirts and hooded sweatshirts, while the girls went for tight jerseys and oversized pullovers. There were quite a few preppies, a fair number of grungeheads, a crew of heavy-metal death rockers, a squadron of hopeless nerds, some suburban homeboys, and a smattering of die-hard punks. In all of Winwood High School, though, I was the only student in a Catholic school uniform, and it made me kind of exotic.

As part of my ongoing campaign to convince my mother to let me transfer to Immaculate Mary, I wore my uniform every day for a whole month. She hassled me about it for the first week or so, but finally just threw up her hands.

"Go ahead," she told me. "Wear whatever you want. As far as I'm concerned you can get married in that stupid uniform. But I'm not going to spend a penny to send you to Catholic school."

"It's not that expensive," I protested. "I'll get a part-time job."

"The money's not the issue. It's a matter of principle."

Aside from Paul, Lisa, and maybe Jason, no one at Winwood understood that I was wearing my uniform for a reason. Everyone just thought I was hilarious, especially the boys. Some of them started calling me "Sister Tammy" and making the sign of the cross when they passed me in the hall. Pretty soon lots of people were doing it.

It was my English teacher who finally complained. Miss Benson used to be a nun, and I guess she thought I was making fun of Catholics, even though this was the furthest thing from my mind.

Poor Mr. Hendricks had to call me into his office for another one of our conferences. He seemed to have aged a lot over the past month or so. I noticed a slight tremor in his hand when he reached for his Styrofoam cup.

"Listen," he said, "it's time to retire this getup of yours."

"Why?" I asked, playing dumb. "Have you instituted a dress code?"

He pressed his fingertips to his temples and moved them in circles.

"Don't push me, Tammy. My head feels like someone's been pounding spikes into it."

"I'm wearing a skirt, blouse, and knee socks. Does that violate some sort of regulation?"

"Some people are religious," he told me, "and they don't go for this sort of baloney. So do me a favor and lose the uniform, okay?"

I felt sorry for Mr. Hendricks. If I could have, I would've loved to help him out.

"What happens if I don't?

"You know the drill."

So I wore the uniform the next day and he suspended me for the third time in as many months, supposedly for "disruptive behavior." My mother went ballistic.

"You want to go to Catholic school?" she screamed. "Fine. Go to Catholic school. But don't come crying to me when they start whacking you with a ruler."

MR. M.

THE FIRST REPORTER called during dinner. She was from the *West Plains Herald,* and could barely conceal her excitement.

"Mr. McAllister, is it true you tried to steal a high school election?"

"No comment," I said, and hung up the phone.

It rang again a few seconds later.

"One question, sir. Could you explain your hatred of Tracy Flick?"

"I don't hate her," I said, and hung up again. This time I pulled out the jack.

So at least I had some advance warning. It saved me from being completely blindsided when the next morning's paper thudded onto my doorstep with a picture of Tracy smiling up from the front page. I stood on the porch in my robe and slippers, and read the article — "Scandal Mars School Election" — with the most powerful sense of unreality I'd ever experienced:

> *Students and faculty at Winwood High were stunned today by reports that a popular teacher reportedly tried to rig yesterday's election for President of the Student Government Association.*
>
> *"This is America," said one tearful junior, who asked not to be identified. "This isn't supposed to happen here."*
>
> *According to a highly placed administrator at the school, the teacher, James T. McAllister, allegedly dumped an undisclosed number of ballots into a trash can in order to ensure the election of his own hand-picked candidate. The fraud would have gone undetected but for an eagle-eyed janitor who discovered the missing ballots during a routine cleanup.*
>
> *"It was pure luck," said Joseph Delvecchio, the fifty-four-year-old custodian who made the surpris-*

ing discovery. "Otherwise he would have got away with it."

McAllister's motives in the alleged vote-tampering incident remain unclear. In a brief interview with the Herald, *the popular history teacher denied widespread rumors that he bore a long-standing grudge against Tracy Flick, 17, who was named President of the Student Government Association today in an early morning ceremony.*

"I don't hate her," McAllister insisted.

School officials refused to comment about potential disciplinary actions aimed at the teacher.

"He's a sensible man," said one administration official. "Maybe he'll do the decent thing and resign."

I must have read the article three times over before looking up. A woman I'd never seen before was standing on the sidewalk in front of my house, waiting for her basset hound to finish shitting on my lawn. She looked me straight in the eye, daring me to object, her mouth curling into a contemptuous smile. I tucked the paper under my arm and went inside.

It only got worse. The story got picked up by the wire services, and for a day or two it was everywhere. Not headline news, but a curiosity, something people could listen to and shake their heads about. NPR used it as one of their human interest squibs. Peter Jennings arched his eyebrows as he reported it, as if to suggest that even he was surprised by this one. The *New York Post* reprinted Tracy's picture, along with the caption "She Wuz Robbed!"

Diane stood by me through the entire ordeal, never once flinching in her support. In a way, I think she was grateful for my humiliation. It sort of evened things out between us, making it easier for her to forgive me for my little fling with Sherry, who didn't even bother to call and say she was sorry to hear about my troubles.

Mercifully, the story had a short life. Riots struck L.A. that same week, and for a long time the country forgot about everything but that. It's awful to admit, but I felt a powerful sense of relief every time I turned on the TV and saw buildings going up in flames, and that poor man being dragged out of his truck.

14

LISA FLANAGAN

PAUL AND I broke up about a month after the election. It wasn't that we stopped liking each other. We just sort of ran out of things to talk about.

The summer that followed was a strange, lonely, oddly exciting time for me. I went running early in the morning, when the world was still damp and cool, then spent the day hanging around the house, reading and watching TV. Three or four nights a week I worked in the Carvel ice cream store in downtown West Plains. That was my entire social life, waiting on customers and goofing around with the other people who worked there.

The only thing that kept me going was the national election, which I followed the way some guys I know follow baseball. A whole new world of information

cracked wide open, one source leading naturally to another—the *Times, The New Republic, The McLaughlin
Group, Crossfire,* Gergen and Shields. There was always
something new to read, another debate to watch, more
expert analysis.

All I lacked was someone to share it with, a friend
who cared about the campaign even half as much as I
did. Sometimes I'd hear about college kids working for
the candidates, and it seemed so vital and glamorous, so
much more significant than crowning a hot fudge sun-
dae with a maraschino cherry. I fantasized constantly
about running away, hopping a Greyhound to Little
Rock to volunteer my services, going sleepless for a good
cause, waking up red-eyed and tongue-sore after licking
envelopes until five in the morning.

My mother was the only person I saw on a regular
basis, and she didn't have a lot to offer in the way of scin-
tillating conversation, at least not the kind I needed. The
political process didn't just bore her, it offended her. I
remember her walking into the living room one night
and staring at the screen for a couple of seconds with an
expression of unmitigated disgust, like she'd caught me
watching pornography.

"Who *is* this guy?" she asked.

"You're joking, right?"

She shook her head. "I see him all the time, but I have
no idea who he is."

"Mom," I said, "what planet are you on? That's Marlin Fitzwater, the President's spokesman."

It amazed me that a grown woman could be so thoroughly clueless. She reminded me of those people who crawl out from under their rocks to sit on the really important juries, the ones who've never seen the Rodney King video and swear they've never heard the name of William Kennedy Smith. Whenever I asked who she was going to vote for, she just shrugged and said it didn't really matter.

"They're all the same."

"They're not the *same,* Mom. Don't you read the papers?"

"Honey," she'd say, "I think you need a boyfriend. When you were with Paul, you were a much nicer person."

I was working at Carvel one night in July, about a week before the Democratic National Convention, when Mr. M. walked into the store. I almost didn't recognize him. In school he'd been a sharp dresser—baggy pants, denim shirts, bright flowered ties. Now he just looked anonymous, a tired man in a rumpled gray suit, generic tie loose around his open collar.

"Lisa," he said, stiffening with surprise. "I didn't know you worked here."

"Just for the summer. It gets me out of the house."

"I know the feeling." He smiled sheepishly and

jerked his thumb over his shoulder. "I'm selling cars now. Over at Griffin Chevrolet."

"Do you like it?"

He thought hard before answering, like no one had ever asked him this before.

"It's okay. Better than I expected. But you really have to hustle."

All at once, I'm not sure why, this wave of embarrassment came washing over me. Our past expanded in that bright cool space until it seemed to be everywhere, like the smell of ice cream. Not just the election or the fact that he'd lost his job, but everything—me and Paul, me and Tammy, things Mr. M. had said in class that I knew I'd never forget.

"Um . . . Can I help you?"

"Vanilla cone," he said. "Sprinkles if you've got them."

"Small, medium, or large?"

"Doesn't matter. Medium, I guess."

I grabbed a wafer cone off the top of the stack and yanked the lever on the soft-serve machine. A rope of ice cream came chugging out. Against store policy, I filled the whole cone, from the bottom up.

"How's Paul?" he asked.

"Okay, I guess."

"You guess?"

"We broke up."

He seemed surprised. Most people reacted that way. Paul and I looked like a great couple to the outside world, but we weren't that great together. After a while, all we really knew how to do with each other was have sex. It got a little tedious.

"I'm sorry to hear it," he said.

"It's okay. We're still friends."

I twirled the cone through the sprinkle tray and passed it over the counter. After I rang up the sale and gave him his change, I realized I wasn't nervous anymore.

Mr. M. pointed at his cone. He ate it like a kid, slurping from the top instead of licking from the bottom.

"Can I buy you one?"

"No, thanks. I'm so sick of ice cream you wouldn't believe it."

He took another slurp. There was a sprinkle attached to his bottom lip.

"Not me. Never get sick of ice cream."

He didn't seem to be in any big hurry to leave. A funny thought popped into my head, something I'd been curious about for a long time.

"Mr. M.," I said, "what's your opinion of George Will?"

"George Will?" He plucked a napkin from the dispenser and wiped his mouth. "What about him?"

"I've been wondering. Do you think he's as smart as he seems?"

"Does he seem smart to you?"

"Very. But there's one thing that bothers me. If he's so smart, why doesn't he run for office?"

Mr. M.'s face lit up with pleasure. I could see him sitting on his desk, tossing a piece of chalk into the air and catching it without looking.

"George Will's a *pundit*," he said, making it sound like that was the lowest form of life in the animal kingdom. "He wouldn't have the guts to run for dogcatcher."

"Why not?"

"Because he'd lose. He's too intellectual. He's an egghead, like Adlai Stevenson."

"Who?"

"Adlai Stevenson. The Democrat who ran against Eisenhower. Read up on him. Then you'll have the answer to your question about George Will."

When he finished his cone, there was no excuse for him to stay any longer. He stuffed his crumpled napkin into the wastebasket and looked up.

"I'm sorry, Lisa. About what happened back there."

"That's okay. You don't have to apologize to me."

"Thanks," he said. "It's nice of you to say that."

The next day I went to the library and checked out a biography of Adlai Stevenson. It was slow going at first, but then I got to like it. All summer long I kept waiting for Mr. M. to come back to Carvel so we could talk about it, but he never showed up.

MR. M.

THE JOB OFFER from Frank Griffin, Jr., came at the perfect time, when I thought I was about to go crazy from boredom and anxiety. I'm just not made for moping around the house. I need to be out in the world—meeting people, asking questions, filling a place in the loud, messy machinery of society.

I'd spent the whole month of May wrestling with the question of what to do with my life. My three most desperate and promising options—teaching English in Japan, relocating to Alaska, applying to law school—all dissolved in the daydream phase, eclipsed by a surprising development: Diane was pregnant. All that hard work had finally paid off.

Our happiness—and we *were* happy, for the first time in recent memory—was edged with a bright border of panic. The economy was rotten. Even if we wanted to sell our house and move someplace cheaper, there was no guarantee we could find a buyer. Diane was hoping to take a year off after the birth, but it was hard to see how we were going to swing that under the present circumstances.

All I really knew was that I needed to find a new job, and find it fast. I spent hours wide awake at night, tormenting myself with worst-case scenarios—I'm a Night Manager at Burger King, ridiculed by my teenage employees; I'm planted in the frozen aisle at the Price Club, gamely offering a tray of microwave stuffed mushrooms to passing shoppers; I'm driving a Mr. Softee truck that plays the same insane jingle over and over, eight hundred times a day.

Frank was a former student of mine, a member of the first class I'd ever taught at Winwood. A completely forgettable kid. From the day he graduated to the night he called, he hadn't crossed my mind a single time.

"Frank Griffin," I said, fruitlessly searching my mind for a face to match the name. "What have you been up to?"

"I'm the sales manager at my father's dealership. Griffin Chevrolet Geo on West Plains Boulevard. That's why I'm calling. I wanted to run something by you."

"What's that?"

"Well, I . . . I heard about your trouble, and I want you to know how sorry I am. You were the best teacher I ever had."

I'd received three or four calls like this from former students, and it's hard for me to explain how good they made me feel. And sad. So much of my identity was still bound up with teaching. It was the only thing I'd ever excelled at.

"Thanks, Frank. I really appreciate your saying that."

"Anyway," he continued, "I'm not sure what you're doing right now, but I was wondering if you'd ever considered sales."

"I haven't," I admitted. "But right now I'm willing to consider anything."

If he heard the implicit insult, he chose to ignore it.

"We're looking for someone," he said. "I think you'd be perfect for the job."

"Why's that?"

"All a good salesman really needs is to listen hard and ask the right questions. It's basically what a teacher does. Just for a different purpose."

So I drove to West Plains the next afternoon, and Frank showed me around the lot. He was a bald, fleshy guy, one of those kids who turned middle-aged the day he received his high-school diploma. I was especially impressed by the Geos, which he told me were more or less identical to Toyotas, but sold for thousands of dollars less.

"It's a smart buy," he said. "All you have to do is give people the wherewithal to see that for themselves."

At the end of the visit, he brought me into a wood-paneled office in the showroom and introduced me to his father. Frank Griffin, Sr., was an imposing figure, large of belly and pink of face, like an old-time machine politician.

"So what do you think?" he asked me. "You want to give it a shot?"

"Sure," I said. "Why not?"

"Great." He stuck out his hand. "Welcome aboard."

I was startled by the suddenness of the agreement, and wanted to make sure they weren't taking me on under false pretenses.

"There's only one problem," I confessed. "I don't know anything about cars."

"Don't worry about it," Frank junior assured me. "You're a smart guy. You'll be up to speed in no time."

He was right, too. I studied the sales material, attended a weekend training seminar, and kept my ears open around the lot. By the end of the summer, I was a thoroughly competent and moderately successful salesman. Sensible cars were my specialty—Prizms, Cavaliers, the Lumina van. I didn't do so well with our sportier models. Something about my personality, I guess.

It's actually kind of exciting. A cheaper high than teaching, but a high nonetheless. There's a lot of psychology involved, and just enough seduction to keep things interesting. You have to know when to talk and when to shut up, when to be a cheerleader and when to play hardball. Diane used to joke that I was getting in touch with my own inner asshole, but all I was really doing was claiming my American birthright. There's a sales professional lying dormant in each and every one of us, just waiting for a chance to blossom.

As long as I'm with customers, I like the job. The only thing I hate is the dead time, hanging around like a vulture waiting for a carcass to turn up. That's when I remember how far I've fallen. When Rudy Francis starts telling nigger jokes and Stan Unfall brags about "porking" his wife. When Frank junior slaps me on the back and calls me "Professor."

That's when I get bitter, when I start wondering how it is that Bill Clinton got to be President and Clarence Thomas got to sit on the Supreme Court, while I ended up here, surrounded by men who have nicknames for their penises, and talk about them like they're old friends. The only difference was that Bill and Clarence lied and I told the truth.

Mostly I keep a low profile around the lot, try to get along with everyone and not make waves. I even kept my mouth shut the other day, when Stan and Rudy defended the rapists from Glen Ridge. The boys were convicted, but the judge gave them such light sentences that the whole process got reduced to a joke. People do more time for possessing a bag of pot than shoving a broomstick up the vagina of a retarded girl. It just makes you crazy to think about it.

"Hey," said Rudy, "she shouldn't have been down there in the first place. What did she think? They wanted to play Monopoly?"

"I hear she had big tits," Stan added, as if this had anything to do with anything. "A major pair of hooters."

I could have said something, but what difference would it have made? Stan and Rudy are grown men. It's too late to shape their minds, to teach them values and a sense of compassion. You have to do that when kids are young, before their personalities harden and they come to love their own ignorance. And besides, what right did I have to be holier-than-thou with anyone? My only consolation was that Frank junior walked away from the conversation, shaking his head in disgust. He was one of mine, and maybe that had made a difference.

TAMMY WARREN

SO MOM WAS WRONG. They don't whack us with rulers at Immaculate Mary. The school's so broke they probably can't afford rulers to whack us with. They also can't afford computers, a gym, or chalk for the blackboards. We even have to supply our own writing paper, believe it or not.

The teachers don't get paid much and sometimes it shows. We have a couple of good ones, fresh out of college, but everyone knows they'll be gone in a year or two, as soon as something better comes along. To make ends meet, my English teacher drives the van that picks us up in the morning. I teased him about it once, and he told me to shut up.

Even though I'm not a Catholic and have no desire to become one, they still make me take the religion class. It's not much of an advertisement for Catholicism, let me tell you. We don't have textbooks and we don't really discuss anything. When the Monsignor's in a bad mood, he just rants and raves for forty-five minutes. When he's in a good mood he runs the class like a quiz show, tossing off easy questions like Alex Trebek in a backwards collar.

"What did Joseph do for a living?"

"Was Jesus Christ a man or was he God?"

The girls laugh behind his back, but no one dares to disagree with him, even when he talks about abortion or premarital sex, subjects that at least a few of my classmates know a lot more about than he does. (Homosexuality doesn't even come up, believe me.) It's almost enough to make me nostalgic for Winwood.

I mean, what was I thinking? Nothing's like what I expected. Wearing my Catholic school uniform to public school was such a *statement*. Wearing it here is just dull. Every day, the same compulsory skirt, blouse, and knee socks. The dopey shoes. Pretty soon I'm going to have to shave my head and pierce my nose just to relieve the boredom.

Dana was my other big disappointment, but I have only myself to blame for that. I got starry-eyed and built her up into something she wasn't. It's a bad habit of mine. I mean, just because someone's sexy and has a cool-looking birthmark, that doesn't mean she can't also be petty and shallow. Madonna, Madonna, Madonna, that's all she ever wants to talk about. Madonna and boys. Mention anything else and she just zones out.

My only good friend is Alice, the freckly redhead I met that first day when I came to visit Dana. Alice is great. I told her all about Lisa a few weeks ago and she didn't freak out or anything. She just asked lots of questions and listened carefully to my answers, like she really wanted to understand. When I explained what happened between Paul and Lisa, she got all indignant on my behalf.

"She was confused," I said. "She didn't know what she wanted."

"Bullshit," she said. "A guy is one thing. But not your *brother*. That's as low as it gets."

I haven't had any contact with Lisa for over a year now. Paul told me she's going to Drew next year to study Political Science. He's going to Rutgers for Liberal Arts.

I'm so jealous of both of them. I wish I could go away too, start all over again someplace better, far away from everyone I've ever known in my entire life.

Because I don't see how I'm going to stand another year of high school.

.

TRACY FLICK

I'D BEEN THINKING about it for a long time, but it took me a whole year to work up the nerve. About a week before graduation, I put on my red dress and drove my mother's beat-up Nova out to the Chevrolet dealership on West Plains Boulevard. The day was blue and balmy, the kind of weather that made me wish I could be a different person, fun-loving and carefree, ready to embrace the moment.

I don't really know what I was after. Revenge, I guess. Maybe an apology. Or maybe just a chance to look him in the eye without my mother present, to let him know I was an adult now, no longer the schoolgirl he'd humiliated and tried to injure. All I knew for sure was that Mr. M. was one of the loose ends I needed to tie up before leaving Winwood for Georgetown.

The approach of graduation had saddened me in a way I hadn't anticipated. The prospect of moving away from my mother, a change I'd craved for as long as I could remember, suddenly filled me with sorrow. We needed to separate, I knew that much, but did the separation have to be sudden and complete? What would she do without me? And where would I find another friend like her?

Brooding over my future, I also found myself second-guessing my past. I grew haunted by the suspicion that I'd let high school slip through my fingers, that for all my accomplishments, I'd missed out on the essential core of the experience.

This revelation had descended upon me a couple of days earlier, at a yearbook-signing party in the cafeteria. Like a tribe of celebrities, the Class of '93 had gathered to swap autographs, reminiscences, and pledges of undying friendship. I arrived with my brand-new *Winwoodian* tucked under my arm, three fresh pens, and a pleasant sense of premature nostalgia.

A half hour later I was devastated. I swear to God, I never felt so empty in my life. Hardly anyone asked me to sign their yearbooks. And when someone did, I was usually stumped, unable to dream up anything the least bit personal or special to say. *I'll never forget Geometry,* I would write. *You were a valued member of the Student Council.*

Other kids didn't seem to share my problem. They wrote to each other in a secret code of friendship, a breezy, intimate language that was as foreign to me as Polish or Swahili: *Don't forget the beanballs, buddy* . . . *Hey Trish, you really know how to dance!* . . . *Catch you on the boardwalk, dude.*

I mean, maybe it wouldn't matter. Maybe two years would pass and no one would remember the beanballs, Trish would be pregnant and miserable, and once inseparable friends would have fallen completely out of touch. But so what? These yearbook sentiments were real, the products of actual friendships my classmates had shared and wanted to preserve, a far cry from the hollow, distant praise hastily composed in my honor: *I'm sure you'll be a great success* . . . *You were a good President* . . . and the ever-popular, *I wish I'd gotten to know you better.*

Late in the party, Paul Warren sat down next to me and we traded books. I opened his to the page with my picture on it, only to find that Mark Fawcett had gotten carried away and scribbled the second half of his long, semiliterate message right over my face in bright green ink. You could hardly recognize me beneath his jagged, nearly illegible, exclamation-studded scrawl.

I turned to the cover pages, both front and back, but couldn't find any blank space there, either. Paul had so many close friends, each one with a unique style of penmanship and a different color ink.

So I ended up writing my note on a full-page color picture of the school, as if that squat, ugly building were a better emblem of me than my own face. *Paul,* I wrote, *we really should have been better friends. I think we have a lot in common, don't you? You're one of the most impressive people at Winwood. I'll never forget our election. Will you call me this summer? My number's in the book.* And then I did something that surprised me. I signed it, *Love, Tracy.*

Paul finished writing in my book the same moment I finished writing in his. We traded back and he rushed off to collect another signature without even bothering to read what I'd written. I was nervous and hopeful when I opened my book to the page with his picture, but all he had to offer was a string of platitudes and generic good wishes, capped off by his full signature—*Paul Warren.* That's it. *Paul Warren.* No *Love,* no *Your friend,* no nothing.

MR. M.

IT WAS a slow Tuesday. Instead of hanging around the showroom listening to Stan and Rudy speculate as to which actresses would give the best blow jobs, I drifted over to the Parts Department for my daily chat with Ray Feldman.

Parts is an oasis of calm in the dealership, a dim cubbyhole office separated from the shine and dazzle of the showroom by a plain wooden door. Ray sat at his desk behind the counter, logging in a delivery on his Mac. Classical music hovered softly in the background.

"How was lunch?" he asked, gazing intently at the luminous screen, clicking away at his mouse.

"Not bad. We ordered subs from Nino's. What about you?"

"Tuna salad. Nothing special." He rolled his chair away from the computer and swiveled to face me, a stocky bear of a guy with a neatly trimmed reddish beard. "So how'd it go last night?"

"Not bad. He slept from midnight until close to five."

"Hey." Ray saluted me with a clenched fist and a grin. "All *right*. How's his appetite?"

"Good. Maybe a little too good. Diane's nipples are still pretty sore. She's thinking about switching to formula."

Ray tugged thoughtfully on the short hairs of his beard. "That's okay. There's no law that says you have to breast-feed."

"She wants to, though. She says she loves it, even when it hurts like hell."

He ran a hand down the wrinkled front of his shirt, pausing to caress his belly.

"It must be amazing, Jim. Feeding someone with your own body."

This is what we talked about every day, Ray and I. How much Jason ate and how often. Cloth diapers vs. disposables. Did we put him to sleep on his back or stomach? Everyone at the lot knew about the birth of my son, of course, but only Ray treated it as a subject of enduring interest. Stan and Rudy just wanted to know if I was getting any nooky yet.

"Oh, by the way," he said, "I was wondering if you had a picture."

"Yeah," I laughed. "I showed it to you yesterday, and the day before that, and the day before that."

"Not that one," he said. "One I can keep."

"Oh," I replied, not quite able to conceal my surprise.

"I have pictures of all my friends' kids," he explained, a bit defensively. "I put them up on the fridge with magnets."

All at once, I felt like a fool. Ray was right—we *were* friends; the least I could do was bring him a picture. It seemed crazy that he'd never met my wife and child—people we discussed in detail every day—and equally crazy that I knew next to nothing about his personal life, except that he lived alone and read a lot of mysteries. I had no idea if he had a girlfriend, or was gay, or someday wanted to have children himself.

"Sure," I said. "I'll bring you one tomorrow."

Just then the door burst open behind me, flooding the cubbyhole with light. My colleague Rudy stood grinning in the doorway, a hatchet-faced man in an iridescent blue suit. He cleared his throat and sculpted a sweet pair of hips in the air.

"Mr. McAllister," he said, "there's a customer here to see you."

"Isn't it Stan's turn?"

"She requested you by name," he told me, his voice dripping with insinuation. "If you're busy I'll be happy to attend to her . . . automotive needs."

"It must be the woman who looked at the Camaro last week. She was supposed to get back to me yesterday."

I glanced at Ray on my way out the door. He'd already rolled his chair back up to the computer and resumed his life's work, assigning inventory numbers to air filters and side-view mirrors. Stepping into the showroom, I made a mental note to remember the baby picture.

She was standing with her back to me, admiring a pale green Metro convertible, so I saw the dress before I saw her face. The red of it jolted me like an electric shock. I reached up to straighten my tie, and she turned around in the same instant, smiling in a puzzled sort of way, as if a stranger had spoken her name.

TRACY FLICK

WE MADE an aimless circuit of the lot, stopping every now and then to admire another car—the unreal shine of the paint, the glossy tires, the computer printouts attached to the back windows, each one cluttered with gibberish and a picture of a gas pump.

"This is a Cavalier," he'd say, as if he thought I might secretly be interested in making a purchase. "Basic transportation at a basic price. But a little sportier than you might expect."

I'd nod solemnly, doing my best imitation of a serious customer, my mind suddenly empty of the insults and accusations I'd been hoarding so long for just this occasion. It all seemed irrelevant now—the election, Mr. M.'s treachery, all those nights I'd spent wide awake, dreaming of revenge. I was about to graduate. He sold Chevrolets. High school was over for both of us.

"This is the Lumina," he told me. "It's a midsized family sedan. We sell a van in the same model line."

Mr. M. swept his arm in a wide arc over the hood of the car, like Vanna White drawing your attention to more fabulous prizes. He looked older than I remembered, grayer around the temples, more tired in the eyes. I liked his suit, though. It was gray and fashionably cut, and it made him seem like a more serious person than he'd been as a teacher, someone with weight and stature in the adult world.

"Where do they get these names?" I asked. "Who makes them up?"

His eyes crinkled into a squint. "People in Detroit, I guess. Engineers. Marketing types."

"You'd think they could do a little better than 'Lumina.' It's not even a real word."

He nodded. "Cars used to be named for animals and places, but now they've got these crazy made-up names. The Japanese are the worst. I mean, what the heck's a Camry?"

"I don't know," I admitted, wishing that I could impress him with the correct answer.

I looked up and something connected between us. I guess we both realized how absurd it was, after everything that had happened, for the two of us to be standing in a parking lot, surrounded by new cars, wondering what a Camry was. But instead of smiling he suddenly turned serious, the way Jack used to right before he kissed me.

"So tell me," he said. "How was your senior year?"

"Okay."

"That's it? Just okay?"

"Not that great, actually."

"Really?" He licked his fingertip and rubbed at a spot on the Lumina's hood. The car was cherry red, a sexy lipstick color. Sunlight flared off the glass and metal. "Why was that?"

"I don't know. I guess I just wanted it to be over. These last couple of months really seemed to drag."

Mr. M. jingled some change in his pocket and studied the ground. I had a feeling he was going to ask me about Jack.

"Did you go to the prom?"

I shook my head, a little irritated by the question. It really wasn't any of his business.

"I used to chaperone," he told me. "I always enjoyed it. Seeing all these kids turning into men and women before your eyes. It's really something."

Well, thanks a lot, I thought. *Thanks for letting me know what I missed out on.* I'd really wanted to go, but nobody asked me. I even called Larry DiBono at Lehigh to try and convince him to be my date, but he said his girlfriend would kill him if he went out with someone else, even as a friend.

My mom tried to lift my spirits. She insisted that we get all dressed up on prom night and go out to dinner at a fancy restaurant, but the whole thing turned out to be a disaster. We had a stupid argument and both ended up crying in the car on the way home.

"Do you miss teaching?" I just blurted it out, apropos of nothing, in a voice too loud for the distance between us.

He twisted his head and looked over his shoulder for a couple of seconds. I followed his gaze, but there was nothing behind him except for more new cars, impossibly bright and clean in the afternoon sunshine, and a line of these goofy pennants flapping in the breeze. When he turned around, his face revealed nothing.

"Every day," he told me.

After that, we didn't say much. On our way back to the showroom we wandered past the Geos, and I couldn't help stopping to admire those little convertibles. I had this vision of myself cruising through town on a summer evening with the top down, giving people something new to remember me by.

"That's the Metro," he told me. "The most affordable convertible on the market."

"It's so cute. I just want to hop in and drive away."

"No problem," he said. "I'll go get the keys."

MR. M.

"WHERE TO?" she asked.

"Anywhere you want," I told her. "Just as long as we're back in a half hour."

She grinned. "I can't believe we're doing this."

She worked the shifter into first gear, and we lurched out of the lot into the flowing afternoon traffic. It was perfect convertible weather, warm and bright, with just enough breeze to ruffle your hair.

"I wish I'd known," she said, raising her voice to compete with the noise of the wind and the engine. "I would've brought my sunglasses."

We cruised all the way down West Plains Boulevard into Winwood, then took the familiar left turn onto Central. Tracy kept glancing at me as she shifted gears, checking my face for signs of alarm.

I knew where she was taking me, of course, and if my expression remained inscrutable, it was only because I was feeling so many different things at once, not all of them simple or unpleasant. We turned off Central onto Monroe.

"I hope you don't mind," she said. "I have to get something out of my locker."

We took the back way in, the route I'd driven every school day for nine years. We passed the athletic fields, the bleachers empty, the grass parched and trampled. In the distance the school squatted in all its flat stolidity, a dull, two-story structure with nothing to recommend it except the simple, crucial fact that in spite of everything, learning sometimes occurred beneath its roof.

"I haven't been back," I told her. "Not since that morning."

She nodded. "People missed you. Your replacement was a dweeb."

We coasted to a stop at the corner of Sixteenth. The space between us filled with unspoken questions.

"Aren't you worried?" I asked.

"About what?"

"That someone will see us together?"

Her sidelong glance was rich with contempt. For the first time that afternoon I caught a glimpse of the old Tracy, the girl whose ballots I'd crumpled.

"I'm gone," she said. "I don't care what anyone around here thinks anymore."

Gene Sperigno and Adele Massing happened to walk out of main entrance as we drove past. They'd taught math in adjacent classrooms for ten years before falling in love and deciding to get married. I'd sprained my ankle dancing at their wedding. I slouched in the passenger seat, hoping they wouldn't notice me, but it's hard not to be noticed in a lemon-yellow convertible driven by a pretty girl in a blood-red dress. They waved in a puzzled slow motion, and I had no choice but to raise my arm in reply.

Tracy turned into the lot, and we bounced over a series of speed bumps before pulling to a stop in a No Parking zone near the side entrance.

"You can't park here," I told her.

She gave me another one of her looks. "I'm the school President," she said, shutting off the engine and yanking on the emergency brake. "Besides, I'll only be a minute. You want to come in with me?"

"No thanks. I'll wait here."

She disappeared into the building, and I slouched even further in my seat, dreading the possibility that one of my former colleagues would spot me in that wildly conspicuous, illegally parked car, and feel an obligation to say hello. Tracy wasn't the only one who wished she'd brought sunglasses.

To distract me from the all-too-real prospect of a conversation with Walt Hendricks, my mind seized upon a more dramatic and wildly improbable scenario. *A gun,* I told myself. *She's going to get a gun. She's going to close her locker, walk back out to the car, and start shooting.*

I laughed at the thought, but then decided to run with it. Why not? This was America, 1993. All over the country, people were shooting each other for reasons less valid and interesting than the reason Tracy would have for shooting me. It gave me a certain grim satisfaction to imagine the look on her face as she pulled the trigger, to toy with the thought that this was how it might end for me, in a yellow convertible in a high school parking lot, a thirty-three-year-old car salesman dead at the hands of a girl he'd wronged. Great material for a TV movie.

The fantasy was so compelling I have to admit to being almost disappointed when she returned a couple of minutes later, carrying a white book in her hand instead of a weapon. She climbed back into the driver's seat, her expression hovering somewhere between sheepish and amused.

"It may seem strange," she said, "but I was wondering if you would sign this for me."

She held out the yearbook and I took it from her hand, the first *Winwoodian* in a decade that didn't contain my picture. A romanticized pen-and-ink drawing graced the cover, a dreamy vision of Winwood High floating on a bank of clouds, heaven as a school.

"Sure," I said. "Where should I sign?"

She reached across the gearshift and flipped open the cover. Two blank pages stared back at me, a formidable expanse of white.

"Right here's fine," she said, dropping a brand-new Rolling Writer into the crease between the pages. "Take as much room as you want."

I picked up the pen and stared at the emptiness I was supposed to fill with ink, fighting an urge to flip through the book, revisiting the faces of the people who'd vanished from my life, catching up on a year's worth of Winwood history — who had fallen in love and who had broken up, who was going where for college, who said what crazy thing in the cafeteria.

"I really like yearbooks," I told her.

She didn't answer. A minute went by, maybe two. I had no idea where to start or how to finish. It seemed to me then that I could cover every page of the yearbook with paragraph after paragraph of explanation and apology, and still not be any closer to saying the things that needed to be said.

"I'm scared," she whispered. "What if I'm not ready for college?"

"You'll be fine," I told her.

"You think so?"

"Tracy," I said. "You were ready for college three years ago."

More time passed. She drummed her fingers on the steering wheel. I thought of Stan and Rudy waiting in the showroom, pointing at their watches, snorting with delight at our continued absence. I thought of Ray sitting in front of his computer, and reminded myself again to bring him a picture of Jason. Then I uncapped the pen, took a deep breath to clear my head, and started writing.